GRIMM'S FAIRY TALES

Inspiring | Educating | Creating | Entertaining

Brimming with creative inspiration, how-to projects, and useful information to enrich your everyday life, Quarto Knows is a favorite destination for those pursuing their interests and passions. Visit ou site and dig deeper with our books into your area of interest: Quarto Creates, Quarto Cooks, Quarto Homes, Quarto Lives, Quarto Drives, Quarto Explores, Quarto Gifts, or Quarto Kids.

Illustrations
Yann Legendre
www.yannlegendre.com

Cover Design
Sussner Design Co.
www. Sussner.com

Book Design
Lance Rutter

Printed in China

This reimagined edition of the classic favorite features 20 tales by the Brothers Grimm. Each tale is accompanied by lush illustrations from Yann Legendre. His surreal, sometimes haunting, portrayals of the characters in Grimm's tales are bold and utterly captivating, adding a new depth to these classic characters.

This is just one in a new series of books from Rockport Publishers. Classics Reimagined is a library of stunning collector's editions of classic novels illustrated by graphic artists and illustrators from around the world. Each artist offers his or her own unique, visual interpretation of the most well-loved, widely read, and avidly collected literature from renowned authors. From *The Wonderful Wizard of Oz* to *Sherlock Holmes*, and from *Grimm's Fairy Tales* to selected works from Edgar Allan Poe, art lovers and book collectors alike will not be able to resist owning the whole collection.

Also available
The Wonderful Wizard of Oz
978-1-59253-899-7

Alice's Adventures in Wonderland
978-1-63159-369-7

Edgar Allen Poe
978-1-63159-370-3

Pride and Prejudice
978-1-63159-371-0

GRIMM'S FAIRY TALES

BY JACOB AND WILHELM GRIMM

ILLUSTRATED BY YANN LEGENDRE

ORNAMENTS AND BORDERS BY LANCE RUTTER

ROCKPORT

TABLE OF CONTENTS

FOR...

my friend and great artist, Lance Rutter, who jumped into this project without hesitation, knowing how gigantic the work would be.

my publisher, for the trust they put in me from the begining, and for allowing me the freedom to create.

my wife, Stacey, for her immense patience and support.

— YL —

THE FOX AND THE CAT

It happened that the cat met Mr. Fox in the woods. She thought, "He is intelligent and well experienced, and is highly regarded in the world," so she spoke to him in a friendly manner, "Good-day, my dear Mr. Fox. How is it going? How are you? How are you getting by in these hard times?"

The fox, filled with arrogance, examined the cat from head to feet, and for a long time did not know whether he should give an answer. At last he said, "Oh, you poor beard-licker, you speckled fool, you hungry mouse hunter, what are you thinking? Have you the nerve to ask how I am doing? What do you know? How many tricks do you understand?"

"I understand but one," answered the cat, modestly.

"What kind of a trick is it?" asked the fox.

"When the dogs are chasing me, I can jump into a tree and save myself."

"Is that all?" said the fox. "I am master of a hundred tricks, and in addition to that I have a sackful of cunning. I feel sorry for you. Come with me, and I will teach you how one escapes from the dogs."

Just then a hunter came by with four dogs. The cat jumped nimbly up a tree, and sat down at its top, where the branches and foliage completely hid her.

"Untie your sack, Mr. Fox, untie your sack," the cat shouted to him, but the dogs had already seized him, and were holding him fast.

"Oh, Mr. Fox," shouted the cat. "You and your hundred tricks are left in the lurch. If you had been able to climb like I can, you would not have lost your life."

CINDERELLA

A rich man's wife became sick, and when she felt that her end was drawing near, she called her only daughter to her bedside and said, "Dear child, remain pious and good, and then our dear God will always protect you, and I will look down on you from heaven and be near you." With this she closed her eyes and died.

The girl went out to her mother's grave every day and wept, and she remained pious and good. When winter came the snow spread a white cloth over the grave, and when the spring sun had removed it again, the man took himself another wife. This wife brought two daughters into the house with her. They were beautiful, with fair faces, but evil and dark hearts. Times soon grew very bad for the poor stepchild. "Why should that stupid goose sit in the parlor with us?" they said. "If she wants to eat bread, then she will have to earn it. Out with this kitchen maid!"

They took her beautiful clothes away from her, dressed her in an old gray smock, and gave her wooden shoes. "Just look at the proud princess! How decked out she is!" they shouted and laughed as they led her into the kitchen.

There she had to do hard work from morning until evening, get up before daybreak, carry water, make the fires, cook, and wash. Besides this, the sisters did everything imaginable to hurt her. They made fun of her, scattered peas and lentils into the ashes for her, so that she had to sit and pick them out again. In the evening when she had worked herself weary, there was no bed for her. Instead she had to sleep by the hearth in the ashes. And because she always looked dusty and dirty, they called her Cinderella.

One day it happened that the father was going to the fair, and he asked his two stepdaughters what he should bring back for them. "Beautiful dresses," said the one. "Pearls and jewels," said the other. "And you, Cinderella," he said, "what do you want?" "Father, break off for me the first twig that brushes against your hat on your way home."

So he bought beautiful dresses, pearls, and jewels for his two step-daughters. On his way home, as he was riding through a green thicket, a hazel twig brushed against him and knocked off his hat. Then he broke off the twig and took it with him. Arriving home, he gave his step-daughters the things that they had asked for, and he gave Cinderella the twig from the hazel bush.

Cinderella thanked him, went to her mother's grave, and planted the branch on it, and she wept so much that her tears fell upon it and watered it. It grew and became a beautiful tree. Cinderella went to this tree three

times every day, and beneath it she wept and prayed. A white bird came to the tree every time, and whenever she expressed a wish, the bird would throw down to her what she had wished for.

Now it happened that the king pro-claimed a festival that was to last three days. All the beautiful young girls in the land were invited, so that his son could select a bride for himself. When the two stepsisters heard that they too had been invited, they were in high spirits.

They called Cinderella, say-ing, "Comb our hair for us. Brush our shoes and fasten our buckles. We are going to the festi-val at the king's castle." Cinderella obeyed, but wept, because she too would have liked to go to the dance with them. She begged her step-mother to allow her to go.

"You, Cinderella?" she said. "You, all covered with dust and dirt, and you want to go to the festival? You have neither clothes nor shoes, and yet you want to dance!" However, because

Cinderella kept asking, the step-mother finally said, "I have scattered a bowl of lentils into the ashes for you. If you can pick them out again in two hours, then you may go with us."

The girl went through the back door into the garden, and called out, "You tame pigeons, you turtledoves, and all you birds beneath the sky, come and help me to gather: The good ones go into the pot, The bad ones go into your crop."

Two white pigeons came in through the kitchen window, and then the turtledoves, and finally all the birds beneath the sky came whirring and swarming in, and lit around the ashes. The pigeons nodded their heads and began to pick, pick, pick, pick. And the others also began to pick, pick, pick, pick. They gathered all the good grains into the bowl.

Hardly one hour had passed before they were finished, and they all flew out again. The girl took the bowl to her stepmother, and was happy, thinking that now she would be allowed to go to the festival with them. But the stepmother said, "No, Cinderella, you have no clothes, and you don't know how to dance. Everyone would only laugh at you."

Cinderella began to cry, and then the stepmother said, "You may go if you are able to pick two bowls of lentils out of the ashes for me in one hour," thinking to herself, "She will never be able to do that."

The girl went through the back door into the garden, and called out, "You tame pigeons, you turtledoves, and all you birds beneath the sky, come and help me to gather: The good ones go into the pot, The bad ones go into your crop."

Two white pigeons came in through the kitchen window, and then the turtledoves, and finally all the birds beneath the sky came whirring and swarming in, and lit around the ashes. The pigeons nodded their heads and began to pick, pick, pick, pick. And the others also began to pick, pick, pick, pick. They gathered all the good grains into the bowls.

Before a half hour had passed they were finished, and they all flew out again. The girl took the bowls to her stepmother, and was happy, thinking that now she would be allowed to go to the festival with them.

But the stepmother said, "It's no use. You are not coming with us, for you have no clothes, and you don't know how to dance. We would be ashamed of you." With this she turned her back on Cinderella, and hurried away with her two proud daughters.

Now that no one else was at home, Cinderella went to her mother's grave beneath the hazel tree, and cried out: Shake and quiver, little tree, Throw gold and silver down to me. Then the bird threw a gold and silver dress down to her, and slippers embroidered with silk and silver. She quickly put on the dress and went to the festival.

Her stepsisters and her stepmother did not recognize her. They thought she must be a foreign princess, for she looked so beautiful in the golden dress. They never once thought it was Cinderella, for they thought that she was sitting at home in the dirt, looking for lentils in the ashes.

The prince approached her, took her by the hand, and danced with her. Furthermore, he would dance with no one else. He never let go of her hand, and whenever anyone else came and asked her to dance, he would say, "She is my dance partner."

She danced until evening, and then she wanted to go home. But the prince said, "I will go along and escort you," for he wanted to see to whom the beautiful girl belonged. However, she eluded him and jumped into the pigeon coop. The prince waited until her father came, and then he told him that the unknown girl had jumped into the pigeon coop.

The old man thought, "Could it be Cinderella?" He had them bring him an ax and a pick so that he could break the pigeon coop apart, but no one was inside.

When they got home Cinderella was lying in the ashes, dressed in her dirty clothes. A dim little oil-lamp was burning in the fireplace. Cinderella had quickly jumped down from the back of the pigeon coop and had run to the hazel tree. There she had taken off her beautiful clothes and laid them on the grave, and the bird had taken them away again. Then, dressed in her gray smock, she had returned to the ashes in the kitchen.

The next day when the festival began anew, and her parents and her stepsisters had gone again, Cinderella went to the hazel tree and said: Shake and quiver, little tree, Throw gold and silver down to me. Then the bird threw down an even more magnificent dress than on the preceding day.

When Cinderella appeared at the festival in this dress, everyone was astonished at her beauty. The prince had waited until she came, then immediately took her by the hand, and danced only with her. When others came and asked her to dance with them, he said, "She is my dance partner."

When evening came she wanted to leave, and the prince followed her, wanting to see into which house she went. But she ran away from him and into the garden behind the house. A beautiful tall tree stood there, on which hung the most magnificent pears. She climbed as nimbly as a squirrel into the branches, and the prince did not know where she had gone.

He waited until her father came, then said to him, "The unknown girl has eluded me, and I believe she has climbed up the pear tree.

The father thought, "Could it be Cinderella?" He had an ax brought to him and cut down the tree, but no one was in it. When they came to the kitchen, Cinderella was lying there in the ashes as usual, for she had jumped down from the other side of the tree, had taken the beautiful dress back to the bird in the hazel tree, and had put on her gray smock.

On the third day, when her parents and sisters had gone away, Cinderella went again to her mother's grave and said to the tree: Shake and quiver, little tree, Throw gold and silver down to me. This time the bird threw down to her a dress that was more splendid and magnificent than any she had yet had, and the slippers were of pure gold.

When she arrived at the festival in this dress, everyone was so astonished that they did not know what to say. The prince danced only with her, and whenever anyone else asked her to dance, he would say, "She is my dance partner."

When evening came Cinderella wanted to leave, and the prince tried to escort her, but she ran away from him so quickly that he could not follow her. The prince, however, had set a trap. He had had the entire stairway smeared with pitch. When she ran down the stairs, her left slipper stuck in the pitch. The prince picked it up. It was small and dainty, and of pure gold.

The next morning, he went with it to the man, and said to him, "No one shall be my wife except for the one whose foot fits this golden shoe."

The two sisters were happy to hear this, for they had pretty feet. With her mother standing by, the older one took the shoe into her bedroom to try it on. She could not get her big toe into it, for the shoe was too small for her. Then her mother gave her a knife and said, "Cut off your toe. When you are queen you will no longer have to go on foot."

The girl cut off her toe, forced her foot into the shoe, swallowed the pain, and went out to the prince. He took her on his horse as his bride and rode away with her. However, they had to ride past the grave, and there, on the hazel tree, sat the two pigeons, crying out:

Rook di goo, rook di goo!
There's blood in the shoe.
The shoe is too tight,
This bride is not right!

Then he looked at her foot and saw how the blood was running from it.

He turned his horse around and took the false bride home again, saying that she was not the right one, and that the other sister should try on the shoe.

She went into her bedroom, and got her toes into the shoe all right, but her heel was too large. Then her mother gave her a knife, and said, "Cut a piece off your heel. When you are queen you will no longer have to go on foot."

The girl cut a piece off her heel, forced her foot into the shoe, swallowed the pain, and went out to the prince. He took her on his horse as his bride and rode away with her. When they passed the hazel tree, the two pigeons were sitting in it, and they cried out:

Rook di goo, rook di goo!
There's blood in the shoe.
The shoe is too tight,
This bride is not right!

He looked down at her foot and saw how the blood was running out of her shoe, and how it had stained her white stocking all red. Then he turned his horse around and took the false bride home again. "This is not the right one, either," he said. "Don't you have another daughter?"

"No," said the man. "There is only a deformed little Cinderella from my first wife, but she cannot possibly be the bride."

The prince told him to send her to him, but the mother answered, "Oh, no, she is much too dirty. She cannot be seen."

But the prince insisted on it, and they had to call Cinderella. She first washed her hands and face clean, and then went and bowed down before the prince, who gave her the golden shoe. She sat down on a stool, pulled her foot out of the heavy wooden shoe, and put it into the slipper, and it fitted her perfectly.

When she stood up the prince looked into her face, and he recognized the beautiful girl who had danced with him. He cried out, "She is my true bride."

The stepmother and the two sisters were horrified and turned pale with anger. The prince, however, took Cinderella onto his horse and rode away with her. As they passed by the hazel tree, the two white pigeons cried out:

Rook di goo, rook di goo!
No blood's in the shoe.
The shoe's not too tight,
This bride is right!

After they had cried this out, they both flew down and lit on Cinderella's shoulders, one on the right, the other on the left, and remained sitting there.

When the wedding with the prince was to be held, the two false sisters came, wanting to gain favor with Cinderella and to share her good fortune. When the bridal couple walked into the church, the older sister walked on their right side and the younger on their left side, and the pigeons pecked out one eye from each of them. Afterwards, as they came out of the church, the older one was on the left side, and the younger one on the right side, and then the pigeons pecked out the other eye from each of them.

And thus, for their wickedness and falsehood, they were punished with blindness as long as they lived.

THE MOON

In days gone by there was a land where the nights were always dark, and the sky spread over it like a black cloth, for there the moon never rose, and no star shone in the obscurity. At the creation of the world, the light at night had been sufficient.

Three young fellows once went out of this country on a travelling expedition, and arrived in another kingdom, where, in the evening when the sun had disappeared behind the mountains, a shining globe was placed on an oak-tree, which shed a soft light far and wide. By means of this, everything could very well be seen and distinguished, even though it was not so brilliant as the sun. The travellers stopped and asked a countryman who was driving past with his cart, what kind of a light that was.

"That is the moon," answered he; our mayor bought it for three thalers, and fastened it to the oak-tree. He has to pour oil into it daily, and to keep it clean, so that it may always burn clearly. He receives a thaler a week from us for doing it."

When the countryman had driven away, one of them said, "We could make some use of this lamp, we have an oak-tree at home, which is just as big as this, and we could hang it on that. What a pleasure it would be not to have to feel about at night in the darkness!"

"I'll tell you what we'll do," said the second; "we will fetch a cart and horses and carry away the moon. The people here may buy themselves another."

"I'm a good climber," said the third, "I will bring it down."

The fourth brought a cart and horses, and the third climbed the tree, bored a hole in the moon, passed a rope through it, and let it down. When the shining ball lay in the cart, they covered it over with a cloth, that no one might observe the theft. They conveyed it safely into their own country, and placed it on a high oak.

Old and young rejoiced, when the new lamp let its light shine over the whole land, and bed-rooms and sitting-rooms were filled with it. The dwarfs came forth from their caves in the rocks, and the tiny elves in their little red coats danced in rings on the meadows.

The four took care that the moon was provided with oil, cleaned the wick, and received their weekly thaler, but they became old men, and when one of them grew ill, and saw that he was about to die, he appointed that one quarter of the moon, should, as his property, be laid in the grave with him. When he died, the mayor climbed up the tree, and cut off a quarter with the hedge-shears, and this was placed in his coffin. The light of the moon decreased, but still not visibly.

When the second died, the second quarter was buried with him, and the light diminished. It grew weaker still after the death of the third, who likewise took his part of it away with him; and when the fourth was borne to his grave, the old state of darkness recommenced, and whenever the people went out at night without their lanterns they knocked their heads together.

When, however, the pieces of the moon had united themselves together again in the world below, where darkness had always prevailed, it came to pass that the dead became restless and awoke from their sleep. They were astonished when they were able to see again; the moonlight was quite sufficient for them, for their eyes had become so weak that they could not have borne the brilliance of the sun.

They rose up and were merry, and fell into their former ways of living. Some of them went to the play and to dance, others hastened to the public-houses, where they asked for wine, got drunk, brawled, quarreled, and at last took up cudgels, and belabored each other. The noise became greater and greater, and at last reached even to heaven.

Saint Peter who guards the gate of heaven thought the lower world had broken out in revolt and gathered together the heavenly troops, which are to drive back the Evil One when he and his associates storm the abode of the blessed. As these, however, did not come, he got on his horse and rode through the gate of heaven, down into the world below. There he reduced the dead to subjection, bade them lie down in their graves again, took the moon away with him, and hung it up in heaven.

THE SIX SWANS

A king was once hunting in a great forest, and he chased his prey so eagerly that none of his men could follow him. As evening approached he stopped and looked around, and saw that he was lost. He looked for a way out of the woods, but he could not find one. Then he saw an old woman with a bobbing head who approached him. She was a witch.

"My dear woman," he said to her, "can you show me the way through the woods?"

"Oh, yes, your majesty," she answered, "I can indeed. However, there is one condition, and if you do not fulfill it, you will never get out of these woods, and will die here of hunger."

"What sort of condition is it?" asked the king.

"I have a daughter," said the old woman, "who is as beautiful as anyone you could find in all the world, and who well deserves to become your wife. If you will make her your queen, I will show you the way out of the woods."

The king was so frightened that he consented, and the old woman led him to her cottage, where her daughter was sitting by the fire. She received the king as if she had been expecting him. He saw that she was very beautiful, but in spite of this he did not like her, and he could not look at her without secretly shuddering.

After he had lifted the girl onto his horse, the old woman showed him the way, and the king arrived again at his royal castle, where the wedding was celebrated.

The king had been married before, and by his first wife he had seven children, six boys and one girl. He loved them more than anything else in the world. Fearing that the stepmother might not treat them well, even do them harm, he took them to a secluded castle which stood in the middle of a forest. It was so well hidden, and the way was so difficult to find, that he himself would not have found it, if a wise woman had not given him a ball of magic yarn. Whenever he threw it down in front of him, it would unwind itself and show him the way.

However, the king went out to his dear children so often that the queen took notice of his absence. She was curious and wanted to know what he was doing out there all alone in the woods. She gave a large sum of money to his servants, and they revealed the secret to her. They also told her about the ball of yarn which could point out the way all by itself.

She did not rest until she discovered where the king kept the ball of yarn. Then she made some little shirts of white silk. Having learned the art of witchcraft from her mother, she sewed a magic charm into each one of them. Then one day when the king had ridden out hunting, she took the little shirts and went into the woods. The ball of yarn showed her the way.

The children, seeing that someone was approaching from afar, thought that their dear father was coming to them. Full of joy, they ran to meet him. Then she threw one of the shirts over each of them, and when the shirts touched their bodies they were transformed into swans, and they flew away over the woods.

The queen went home very pleased, believing that she had gotten rid of her stepchildren. However, the girl had not run out with her brothers, and the queen knew nothing about her. The next day the king went to visit his children, but he found no one there but the girl.

"Where are your brothers?" asked the king.

"Oh, dear father," she answered, "they have gone away and left me alone." Then she told him that from her window she had seen how her brothers had flown away over the woods as swans. She showed him the feathers that they had dropped into the courtyard, and which she had gathered up.

The king mourned, but he did not think that the queen had done this wicked deed. Fearing that the girl would be stolen away from him as well, he wanted to take her away with him, but she was afraid of her step-mother and begged the king to let her stay just this one more night in the castle in the woods.

The poor girl thought, "I can no longer stay here. I will go and look for my brothers." And when night came she ran away and went straight into the woods. She walked the whole night long without stopping, and the next day as well, until she was too tired to walk any further. Then she saw a hunter's hut and went inside.

She found a room with six little beds, but she did not dare to get into one of them. Instead she crawled under one of them and lay down on the hard ground where she intended to spend the night.

The sun was about to go down when she heard a rushing sound and saw six swans fly in through the window. Landing on the floor, they blew on one another, and blew all their feathers off. Then their swan-skins came off just like shirts. The girl looked at them and recognized her brothers. She was happy and crawled out from beneath the bed. The brothers were no less happy to see their little sister, but their happiness did not last long.

"You cannot stay here," they said to her. "This is a robbers' den. If they come home and find you, they will murder you."

"Can't you protect me?" asked the little sister.

"No," they answered. "We can take

off our swan-skins for only a quarter hour each evening. Only during that time do we have our human forms. After that we are again transformed into swans."

Crying, the little sister said, "Can you not be redeemed?"

"Alas, no," they answered. "The conditions are too difficult. You would not be allowed to speak or to laugh for six years, and in that time you would have to sew together six little shirts from asters for us. And if a single word were to come from your mouth, all your work would be lost."

After the brothers had said this, the quarter hour was over, and they flew out the window again as swans.

Nevertheless, the girl firmly resolved to redeem her brothers, even if it should cost her her life. She left the hunter's hut, went to the middle of the woods, seated herself in a tree, and there spent the night. The next morning she went out and gathered asters and began to sew. She could

not speak with anyone, and she had no desire to laugh. She sat there, looking only at her work.

After she had already spent a long time there it happened that the king of the land was hunting in these woods. His huntsmen came to the tree where the girl was sitting. They called to her, saying, "Who are you?" But she did not answer.

"Come down to us," they said. "We will not harm you."

She only shook her head. When they pressed her further with questions, she threw her golden necklace down to them, thinking that this would satisfy them. But they did not stop, so she then threw her belt down to them, and when this did not help, her garters, and then—one thing at a time—everything that she had on and could do without, until finally she had nothing left but her shift.

The huntsmen, however, not letting themselves be dissuaded, climbed the tree, lifted the girl down, and took her to the king. The king asked, "Who are you? What are you doing in that tree?"

But she did not answer. He asked her in every language that he knew, but she remained as speechless as a fish. Because she was so beautiful, the king's heart was touched, and he fell deeply in love with her. He put his cloak around her, lifted her onto his horse in front of himself, and took her to his castle. There he had her dressed in rich garments, and she glistened in her beauty like bright daylight, but no one could get a word from her.

At the table he seated her by his side, and her modest manners and courtesy pleased him so much that he said, "My desire is to marry her, and no one else in the world." A few days later they were married.

Now the king had a wicked mother who was dissatisfied with this marriage and spoke ill of the young queen. "Who knows," she said, "where the girl who cannot speak comes from? She is not worthy of a king."

A year later, after the queen had brought her first child into the world, the old woman took it away from her while she was asleep, and smeared her mouth with blood. Then she went to the king and accused her of being a cannibal. The king could not believe this, and would not allow anyone to harm her. She, however, sat the whole time sewing on the shirts, and caring for nothing else. The next time, when she again gave birth to a beautiful boy, the deceitful mother-in-law did the same thing again, but the king could not bring himself to believe her accusations. He said, "She is too pious and good to do anything like that. If she were not speechless, and if she could defend herself, her innocence would come to light."

But when the old woman stole away a newly born child for the third time, and accused the queen, who did not defend herself with a single word, the king had no choice but to bring her to justice, and she was sentenced to die by fire.

When the day came for the sentence to be carried out, it was also the last day of the six years during which she had not been permitted to speak or to laugh, and she had thus delivered her dear brothers from the magic curse. The six shirts were finished. Only the left sleeve of the last one was missing. When she was led to the stake, she laid the shirts on her arm. Standing there, as the fire was about to be lighted, she looked around, and six swans came flying through the air. Seeing that their redemption was near, her heart leapt with joy.

The swans rushed towards her, swooping down so that she could throw the shirts over them. As soon as the shirts touched them their swan-skins fell off, and her brothers stood before her in their own bodies, vigorous and handsome. However, the youngest was missing his left arm. In its place he had a swan's wing.

They embraced and kissed one another. Then the queen went to the king, who was greatly moved, and she began to speak, saying, "Dearest husband, now I may speak and reveal to you that I am innocent, and falsely accused."

Then she told him of the treachery of the old woman who had taken away their three children and hidden them.

Then to the king's great joy they were brought forth. As a punishment, the wicked mother-in-law was tied to the stake and burned to ashes. But the king and the queen with her six brothers lived many long years in happiness and peace.

THE DEATH OF THE LITTLE HEN

One time the little hen and the little rooster went to Nut Mountain, and they agreed that whoever would find a nut would share it with the other one. Now the little hen found a large, large nut, but—wanting to eat the kernal by herself—she said nothing about it. However, the kernal was so thick that she could not swallow it down. It got stuck in her throat, and fearing that she would choke to death, she cried out, "Little Rooster, I beg you to run as fast as you can to the well and get me some water, or else I'll choke to death."

The little rooster ran to the well as fast as he could, and said, "Well, give me some water, for the little hen is lying on Nut Mountain. She swallowed a large nut kernal and is about to choke to death on it."

The well answered, "First run to the bride, and get some red silk from her."

The little rooster ran to the bride: "Bride, give me some red silk, and I'll give the red silk to the well, and the well will give me some water, and I'll take the water to the little hen who is lying on Nut Mountain. She swallowed a large nut kernal and is about to choke to death on it."

The bride answered, "First run and get my wreath. It got caught on a willow branch."

So the little rooster ran to the willow and pulled the wreath from its branch and took it to the bride, and the bride gave him some red silk, which he took to the well, which gave him some water, and the little rooster took the water to the little hen, but when he arrived, she had already choked to death, and she lay there dead, and did not move at all.

The little rooster was so sad that he cried aloud, and all the animals came to mourn for the little hen. Six mice built a small carriage which was to carry the little hen to her grave. When the carriage was finished, they hitched themselves to it, and the little rooster drove. On the way they met the fox. "Where are you going, little rooster?"

"I'm going to bury my little hen."

"May I ride along?"

"Yes, but you must sit at the rear, because my little horses don't like you too close to the front."

So he sat at the rear, and then the wolf, the bear, the elk, the lion, and all the animals in the forest. They rode on until they came to a brook. "How can we get across?" said the little rooster.

A straw was lying there next to the brook, and he said, "I'll lay myself across, and you can drive over me." But just as the six mice got onto the

straw, it slipped into the water, and the six mice all fell in and drowned.

They did not know what to do, until a coal came and said, "I am large enough. I will lay myself across and you can drive over me."

So the coal laid itself across the water, but unfortunately it touched the water, hissed, and went out; and it was dead.

A stone saw this happen, and wanting to help the little rooster, it laid itself across the water. The little rooster pulled the carriage himself. He nearly reached the other side with the dead little hen, but there were too many others seated on the back of the carriage, and the carriage rolled back, and they all fell into the water and drowned.

Now the little rooster was all alone with the dead little hen. He dug a grave for her and laid her inside. Then he made a mound on top, and sat on it, and grieved there so long that he too died. And then everyone was dead.

THE GIRL WITHOUT HANDS

miller fell slowly but surely into poverty, until finally he had nothing more than his mill and a large apple tree which stood behind it. One day he had gone into the forest to gather wood, where he was approached by an old man, whom he had never seen before, and who said, "Why do you torment yourself with chopping wood? I will make you rich if you will promise me that which is standing behind your mill."

"What can that be but my apple tree?" thought the miller, said yes, and signed it over to the strange man.

The latter, however, laughed mockingly and said, "I will come in three years and get what belongs to me," then went away.

When he arrived home, his wife came up to him and said, "Miller, tell me, where did all the wealth come from that is suddenly in our house? All at once all the chests and boxes are full, and no one brought it here, and I don't know where it came from."

He answered, "It comes from a strange man whom I met in the woods and who promised me great treasures if I would but sign over to him that which stands behind the mill. We can give up the large apple tree for all this."

"Oh, husband!" said the woman, terrified. "That was the devil. He didn't mean the apple tree, but our daughter, who was just then standing behind the mill sweeping the yard."

The miller's daughter was a beautiful and pious girl, and she lived the three years worshipping God and without sin. When the time was up and the day came when the evil one was to get her, she washed herself clean and drew a circle around herself with chalk. The devil appeared very early in the morning, but he could not approach her.

He spoke angrily to the miller, "Keep water away from her, so she cannot wash herself any more. Otherwise I have no power over her."

The miller was frightened and did what he was told. The next morning the devil returned, but she had wept into her hands, and they were entirely clean. Thus he still could not approach her, and he spoke angrily to the miller, "Chop off her hands. Otherwise I cannot get to her."

The miller was horrified and answered, "How could I chop off my own child's hands!"

Then the evil one threatened him, saying, "If you do not do it, then you will be mine, and I will take you yourself."

This frightened the father, and he promised to obey him. Then he went to the girl and said, "My child, if I do not chop off both of your hands, then the devil will take me away, and in my fear I have promised him to do this. Help me in my need, and forgive me of the evil that I am going to do to you."

She answered, "Dear father, do with me what you will. I am your child," and with that she stretched forth both hands and let her father chop them off.

The devil came a third time, but she had wept so long and so much onto the stumps, that they were entirely clean. Then he had to give up, for he had lost all claim to her.

The miller spoke to her, "I have gained great wealth through you. I shall take care of you in splendor as long as you live."

But she answered, "I cannot remain here. I will go away. Compassionate people will give me as much as I need."

Then she had her mutilated arms tied to her back, and at sunrise she set forth, walking the entire day until it was night. She came to a royal garden, and by the light of the moon she saw that inside there were trees full of beautiful fruit. But she could not get inside, for there it was surrounded by water.

Having walked the entire day without eating a bite, she was suffering from hunger, and she thought, "Oh, if only I were inside the garden so I could eat of those fruits. Otherwise I shall perish."

Then she kneeled down and, crying out to God the Lord, she prayed. Suddenly an angel appeared. He closed a head gate, so that the moat dried up, and she could walk through.

She entered the garden, and the angel went with her. She saw a fruit tree with beautiful pears, but they had all been counted. She stepped up to the tree and ate from it with her mouth, enough to satisfy her hunger, but no more. The gardener saw it happen, but because the angel was standing by her he was afraid and thought that the girl was a spirit. He said nothing and did not dare to call

out nor to speak to the spirit. After she had eaten the pear she was full, and she went and lay down in the brush.

The king who owned this garden came the next morning. He counted the fruit and saw that one of the pears was missing. He asked the gardener what had happened to it. It was not lying under the tree, but had somehow disappeared.

The gardener answered, "Last night a spirit came here. It had no hands and ate one of the pears with its mouth."

The king said, "How did the spirit get across the water? And where did it go after it had eaten the pear?"

The gardener answered, "Someone dressed in snow-white came from heaven and closed the head gate so the spirit could walk through the moat. Because it must have been an angel I was afraid, and I asked no questions, and I did not call out. After the spirit had eaten the pear it went away again."

The king said, "If what you said is true, I will keep watch with you tonight."

After it was dark the king entered the garden, bringing a priest with him who was to talk to the spirit. All three sat down under the tree and kept watch. At midnight the girl came creeping out of the brush, stepped up to the tree, and again ate off a pear with her mouth. An angel dressed in white was standing next to her.

The priest walked up to them and said, "Have you come from God, or from the world? Are you a spirit or a human?"

She answered, "I am not a spirit, but a poor human who has been abandoned by everyone except God."

The king said, "Even if you have been abandoned by the whole world, I will not abandon you."

He took her home with him to his royal castle, and because she was so beautiful and pure he loved her with all his heart, had silver hands made for her, and took her as his wife.

After a year the king had to go out into the battlefield, and he left the young queen in the care of his mother, saying, "If she has a child, support her and take good care of her, and immediately send me the news in a letter."

She gave birth to a beautiful son. The old mother quickly wrote this in a letter, giving the joyful news to the king.

Now on the way the messenger stopped at a brook to rest. Tired from his long journey, he fell asleep. Then the devil came to him. He still wanted to harm the pious queen, and he took the letter, putting in its place one that stated that the queen had brought a changeling into the world. When the king read this letter he was frightened and saddened, but nevertheless he wrote an answer that they should take good care of the queen until his return. The messenger returned with this letter, but he rested at the same place, and again fell asleep. The devil came again and placed a different letter in his bag. This letter said that they should kill the queen with her child.

The old mother was terribly frightened when she received this letter. She could not believe it, and wrote to the king again, but she got back the same answer, because each time the devil substituted a false letter. And the last letter even stated that they should keep the queen's tongue and eyes as proof.

The old mother lamented that such innocent blood was to be shed, and in the night she had a doe killed, cut out its tongue and eyes, and had them put aside.

Then she said to the queen, "I cannot have you killed as the king has ordered, but you can no longer stay here. Go out into the wide world with your child, and never come back."

The old mother tied the queen's child onto her back, and the poor woman went away with weeping eyes. She came to a great, wild forest where she got onto her knees and prayed to God. Then the angel of the Lord appeared to her and led her to a small house. On it was a small sign with the words, "Here anyone can live free."

A snow-white virgin came from the house and said, "Welcome, Queen," then led her inside. She untied the small boy from her back, held him to her breast so he could drink, and then laid him in a beautiful made-up bed.

Then the poor woman said, "How did you know that I am a queen?"

The white virgin answered, "I am an angel, sent by God to take care of you and your child."

She stayed in this house for seven years, and was well taken care of. And through the grace of God and her own piety her chopped-off hands grew back.

The king finally came back home from the battlefield, and the first thing he wanted to do was to see his wife and their child.

Then the old mother began to weep, saying, "You wicked man, why did you write to me that I was to put two innocent souls to death," and she showed him the two letters that the evil one had counterfeited. Then she continued to speak, "I did what you ordered," and showed him as proof the eyes and the tongue.

Then the king began to weep even more bitterly for his poor wife and his little son, until the old woman had mercy and said to him, "Be satisfied that she is still alive. I secretly had a doe killed and took the proofs from it. I tied your wife's child onto her back and told her to go out into the wide world, and she had to promise never to come back here, because you were so angry with her."

Then the king said, "I will go as far as the sky is blue, and will neither eat nor drink until I have found my dear wife and my child again, provided that in the meantime they have not died or perished from hunger."

Then the king traveled about for nearly seven years, searching in all the stone cliffs and caves, but he did not find her, and he thought that she had perished. He neither ate nor drank during the entire time, but God kept him alive. Finally he came to a great forest, where he found a little house with a sign containing the words, "Here anyone can live free."

The white virgin came out, took him by the hand, led him inside, and said, "Welcome, King," then asked him where he had come from.

He answered, "I have been traveling about for nearly seven years looking for my wife and her child, but I cannot find them."

The angel offered him something to eat and drink, but he did not take it, wanting only to rest a little. He lay down to sleep, covering his face with a cloth.

Then the angel went into the room where the queen was sitting with her son, whom she normally called "Filled-with-Grief."

The angel said to her, "Go into the next room with your child. Your husband has come."

She went to where he was lying, and the cloth fell from his face.

Then she said, "Filled-with-Grief, pick up the cloth for your father and put it over his face again."

The child picked it up and put it over his face again. The king heard this in his sleep and let the cloth fall again.

Then the little boy grew impatient and said, "Mother, dear, how can I cover my father's face? I have no father in this world. I have learned to pray, 'Our father which art in heaven,' and you have said that my father is in heaven, and that he is our dear God. How can I know such a wild man? He is not my father." Hearing this, the king arose and asked who she was.

She said, "I am your wife, and this is your son Filled-with-Grief."

He saw her living hands and said, "My wife had silver hands."

She answered, "Our merciful God has caused my natural hands to grow back." The angel went into the other room, brought back the silver hands, and showed them to him.

Now he saw for sure that it was his dear wife and his dear child, and he kissed them, and rejoiced, and said, "A heavy stone has fallen from my heart."

Then the angel of God gave them all something to eat, and then they went back home to his old mother. There was great joy everywhere, and the king and the queen conducted their wedding ceremony once again, and they lived happily until their blessed end.

CAT
AND
MOUSE
IN
PARTNERSHIP

A cat had made the acquaintance of a mouse, and had said so much to her about the great love and friendship that he felt for her, that at last the mouse agreed that they should live and keep house together.

"But we must make preparations for winter, or else we shall suffer from hunger," said the cat, "and you, little mouse, cannot venture out everywhere, or in the end you will be caught in a trap."

This good advice was followed, and they bought a pot of fat, but they did not know where to store it. Finally, after much consideration, the cat said, "I know of no place where it will be better stored up than in the church. No one dares take anything away from there. We will put it beneath the altar, and not touch it until we are in need of it."

So the pot was stored safely away, but it was not long before the cat took a great longing for it, and said to the mouse, "I wanted to tell you, little mouse, that my cousin has brought a little son into the world, and she has asked me to be his godfather. He is white with brown spots, and I am to hold him over the baptismal font. Let me go out today, and you look after the house by yourself."

"Yes, yes," answered the mouse. "By all means go, and if you get anything good to eat, think of me. I would like to drink a drop of sweet red christening wine myself."

All this, however, was untrue. The cat had no cousin, and had not been asked to be godfather. He went straight to the church, crept up to the pot of fat, began to lick at it, and licked off the top of the fat. Then he went for a stroll on the roofs of the town, looked out for opportunities, and then stretched out in the sun, licking his whiskers whenever he thought of the pot of fat. He did not return home until it was evening.

"Well, here you are again," said the mouse. "You must have had a happy day."

"Everything went well," answered the cat.

"What name did they give the child?" asked the mouse.

"Top-Off," said the cat quite coolly.

"Top-Off?" cried the mouse. "That is a very odd and uncommon name. Is it a usual one in your family?"

"What does that matter?," said the cat. "It is no worse than Crumb-Thief, as your godchildren are called."

Before long the cat was seized by another fit of longing. He said to the mouse, "You must do me a favor, and once more manage the house alone for a day. I have been asked again to be godfather, and since the child has a white ring around its neck, I cannot refuse."

The good mouse consented. However, the cat crept behind the town wall to the church, and devoured half the pot of fat.

"Nothing tastes as good as that which one eats by oneself," he said, and was quite satisfied with his day's work.

When he arrived home the mouse asked, "What name was this child christened with?"

"Half-Gone," answered the cat.

"Half-Gone? What are you saying? I have never heard that name in all my life. I'll wager it is not in the almanac."

The cat's mouth soon again began to water for the delicious goods. "All good things come in threes," he said to the mouse.

"I have been asked to be godfather again. The child is totally black, only it has white paws. Otherwise it has

not a single white hair on its whole body. This only happens once every few years. You will let me go, won't you?"

"Top-Off. Half-Gone," answered the mouse. "They are such odd names, that they make me stop and think."

"Here you sit at home," said the cat, "with your dark gray fur coat and long braid of hair capturing fantasies. That is because you do not go out in the daytime."

During the cat's absence the mouse cleaned the house, and put it in order, but the greedy cat devoured all the rest of the fat.

"One has peace only after everything is eaten up," he said to himself. Well filled and fat, he did not return home until nighttime. The mouse immediately asked what name had been given to the third child.

"You will not like it either," said the cat. "His name is All-Gone."

"All-Gone!", cried the mouse. "That is the most worrisome name of all. I have never seen it in print. All-Gone! What can that mean?" Then she shook her head, curled herself up, and lay down to sleep.

From this time forth no one invited the cat to be godfather, but when winter had come and there was no longer anything to be found outside, the mouse thought of their stored food, and said, "Come cat, we will go to our pot of fat which we have stored up for ourselves. It will taste good now."

"Yes," answered the cat. "You will enjoy it as much as you would enjoy sticking that dainty tongue of yours out of the window."

They set out on their way, but when they arrived, the pot of fat, to be sure, was still in its place, but it was empty. "Alas," said the mouse, "now I see what has happened. Now it comes to light.

You are a true friend. You ate everything when you were serving as a godfather. First top off, then half done, then ..."

"Be quiet!" cried the cat. "One more word, and I will eat you too."

"All gone" was already on the poor mouse's lips. She had scarcely spoken it before the cat sprang on her, seized her, and swallowed her down. You see, that is the way of the world.

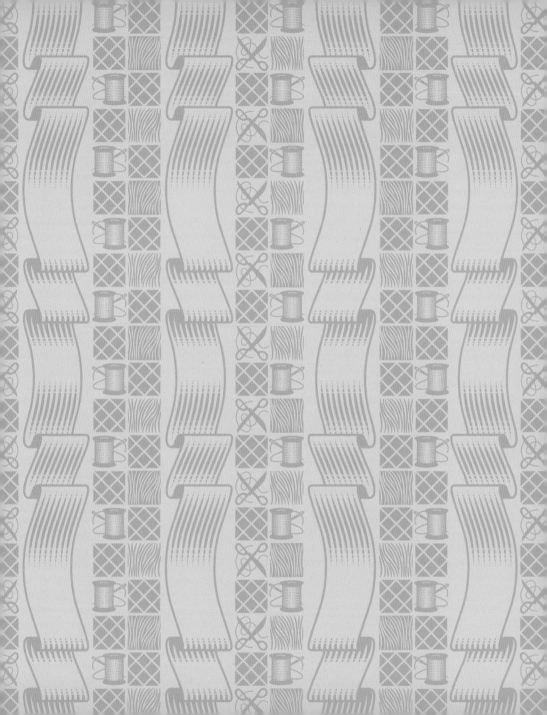

THE
BRAVE
LITTLE
TAILOR

One summer morning a little tailor was sitting on his table near the window. In good spirits, he was sewing with all his might. A peasant woman came down the street crying, "Good jam for sale! Good jam for sale!" That sounded good to the little tailor, so he stuck his dainty head out the window and shouted, "Come up here, my dear woman! You can sell your goods here!"

The woman carried her heavy basket up the three flights of stairs to the tailor, who had her unpack all of her jars. He examined them, picking each one up and holding it to his nose. Finally he said, "This jam looks good to me. Weigh out four ounces for me, even if it comes to a quarter pound."

The woman, who had hoped to make a good sale, gave him what he asked for, then went away angry and grumbling. "May God bless this jam to give me health and strength," said the little tailor. Then taking a loaf of bread from his cupboard, he cut himself a large slice and spread it with the jam. "That is not going to taste bad," he said, "but I will finish the jacket before I bite into it."

He laid the bread aside and continued his sewing, happily making his stitches larger and larger. Meanwhile the smell of the sweet jam rose to the wall where a large number of flies were sitting. Attracted by the smell, a swarm of them settled onto the bread.

"Hey! Who invited you?" said the little tailor, driving away the unbidden guests. However, the flies, who did not understand German, would not be turned away, and they came back in ever-increasing numbers. Finally, losing his temper, he reached for a piece of cloth and shouted, "Wait, now I'm going to give it to you!" then hit at them without mercy. When he backed off and counted, there were no fewer than seven of them lying dead before him, with their legs stretched out.

"Aren't you someone?" he said to himself, surprised at his own bravery. The whole town shall hear about this." He hastily cut out a banner for himself, then embroidered on it with large letters, Seven with one blow. "The town?" he said further. "The whole world shall hear about this!" And his heart jumped for joy like a lamb's tail.

The tailor tied the banner around his body and set forth into the world, for he thought that his workshop was too small for such bravery. Before leaving he looked about his house for something that he could take with him. Finding nothing but a piece of old cheese, he put that into his pocket. Outside the town gate he found a bird that was caught in a bush. It went into his pocket with the cheese.

He bravely took to the road, and being light and agile he did not grow weary. The road led him up a

mountain, and when he reached the top a huge giant was sitting there, looking around contentedly.

The little tailor went up to him cheerfully and said, "Good day, comrade. Are you just sitting here looking at the wide world? I am on my way out there to prove myself. Do you want to come with me?" The giant looked at the tailor with contempt, saying, "You wretch! You miserable fellow!"

"You don't say!" answered the little tailor. Unbuttoning his coat, he showed the banner to the giant. "You can read what kind of man I am." The giant read Seven with one blow, and thinking that the tailor had killed seven men, he gained some respect for the little fellow.

But he did want to put him to the test, so he picked up a stone and squeezed it with his hand until water dripped from it. "Do what I just did," said the giant, "if you have the strength."

"Is that all?" said the little tailor. "That is child's play for someone like me."

SEVEN WITH ONE BLOW

Reaching into his pocket he pulled out the soft cheese and squeezed it until liquid ran from it. "That was even better, wasn't it?" he said.

The giant did not know what to say, for he did not believe the little man. Then the giant picked up a stone and threw it so high that it could scarcely be seen. "Now, you little dwarf, do that."

"A good throw," said the tailor, "but the stone did fall back to earth. I'll throw one for you that will not come back." He reached into his pocket, pulled out the bird, and threw it into the air. Happy to be free, the bird flew up and away, and did not come back. "How did you like that, comrade?" asked the tailor.

"You can throw well enough," said the giant, but now let's see if you are able to carry anything proper." He led the little tailor to a mighty oak tree that had been cut down and was lying on the ground. He said, "If you are strong enough, then help me carry this tree out of the woods."

"Gladly," answered the little man. "You take the trunk on your shoulder, and I will carry the branches and twigs. After all, they are the heaviest."

The giant lifted the trunk onto his shoulder, but the tailor sat down on a branch, and the giant, who could not see behind himself, had to drag long the entire tree, with the little tailor sitting on top. Cheerful and in good spirits, he whistled the song "There Were Three Tailors Who Rode Out to the Gate," as though carrying a tree were child's play.

The giant, after dragging the heavy load a little way, could not go any further, and he called out, "Listen, I have to drop the tree."

The tailor jumped down agilely, took hold of the tree with both arms, as though he had been carrying it, and said to the giant, "You are such a big fellow, and you can't even carry a tree." They walked on together until they came to a cherry tree. The giant took hold of the treetop where the ripest fruit was hanging, bent it down, and put it into the tailor's hand, inviting him to eat. However, the little tailor was much too weak to hold the tree, and when the giant let go, the tree sprang upward, throwing the tailor into the air.

When he fell back to earth, without injury, the giant said, "What? You don't have enough strength to hold that little switch?"

"There is no lack of strength," answered the little tailor. "Do you think that that would be a problem for someone who killed seven with one blow? I jumped over the tree because hunters are shooting down there in the brush. Jump over it yourself, if you can."

The giant made the attempt, but could not clear the tree and got stuck in the branches. So the little tailor kept the upper hand here as well.

The giant said, "If you are such a brave fellow, then come with me to our cave and spend the night with us." The little tailor agreed and followed him. When they reached the cave, other giants were sitting there by a fire. Each one had a roasted sheep in his hand and was eating from it. The little tailor looked around and thought, "It is a lot more roomy here than in my workshop.

The giant showed him a bed and told him to lie down and go to sleep. However, the little tailor found the bed too large, so instead of lying there he crept into a corner. At midnight the giant thought that the little tailor was fast asleep, so he got up, took a large iron bar, and with a single blow smashed the bed in two. He thought he had put an end to the grasshopper.

Early the next morning the giants went into the woods, having completely forgotten the little tailor, when he suddenly approached them cheerfully and boldly. Fearing that he would strike them all dead, the terrified giants ran away in haste.

The little tailor continued on his way, always following his pointed nose. After wandering a long time, he came to the courtyard of a royal

palace, and being tired, he lay down in the grass and fell asleep. While he was lying there people came and looked at him from all sides, and they read his banner, Seven with one blow.

"Oh," they said, "what is this great war hero doing here in the midst of peace? He must be a powerful lord." They went and reported him to the king, thinking that if war were to break out, he would be an important and useful man who at any price should not be allowed to go elsewhere. The king was pleased with this advice, and he sent one of his courtiers to the little tailor to offer him a position in the army, as soon as he woke up.

The messenger stood by the sleeper and waited until he stretched his arms and legs and opened his eyes, and then he delivered his offer. "That is precisely why I came here," answered the little tailor. "I am ready to enter the king's service." Thus he was received with honor and given a special place to live. However, the soldiers were opposed to the little tailor, and wished that he were a thousand miles away. "What will happen," they said among themselves, "if we quarrel with him, and he strikes out against us? Seven of us will fall with each blow. People like us can't stand up to that."

So they came to a decision, and all together they went to the king and asked to be released. "We were not made," they said, "to stand up to a man who kills seven with one blow."

The king was sad that he was going to lose all his faithful servants because of one man, and he wished that he had never seen him. He would like to be rid of him, but he did not dare dismiss him, because he was afraid that he would kill him and all his people and then set himself on the royal throne.

He thought long and hard, and finally found an answer. He sent a message to the little tailor, informing him that because he was such a great war hero he would make him an offer. In a forest in his country there lived two giants who were causing great damage with robbery, murder, pillage, and arson. No one could approach them without placing himself in mortal danger. If he could conquer and kill these two giants, the king would give him his only daughter to wife and half his kingdom for a dowry. Furthermore, a hundred horsemen would go with him for support. "That is something for a man like you," thought the little tailor. "It is not every day that someone is offered a beautiful princess and half a kingdom."

"Yes," he replied. "I shall conquer the giants, but I do not need the hundred horsemen. Anyone who can strike down seven with one blow has no cause to be afraid of two."

The little tailor set forth, and the hundred horsemen followed him. At the edge of the forest, he said to them, "You stay here. I shall take care of the giants myself."

Leaping into the woods, he looked to the left and to the right. He soon saw the two giants. They were lying asleep under a tree, snoring until the branches bent up and down. The little tailor, not lazy, filled both pockets with stones and climbed the tree. Once in the middle of the tree, he slid out on a branch until he was seated right above the sleepers. Then he dropped one stone after another onto one of the giant's chest. For a long time the giant did not feel anything, but finally he woke up, shoved his companion, and said, "Why are you hitting me?"

"You are dreaming," said the other one. "I am not hitting you." They fell asleep again, and the tailor threw a stone at the second one.

"What is this?" said the other one. "Why are you throwing things at me?"

"I am not throwing anything at you," answered the first one, grumbling. They quarreled for a while, but because they were tired, they made peace, and they both closed their eyes again. Then the little tailor began his game again. Choosing his largest stone, he threw it at the first giant with all his strength, hitting him in the chest.

"That is too mean!" shouted the giant,

then jumped up like a madman and pushed his companion against the tree, until it shook. The other one paid him back in kind, and they became so angry that they pulled up trees and struck at each other until finally, at the same time, they both fell to the ground dead.

Then the little tailor jumped down. "It is fortunate," he said, "that they did not pull up the tree where I was sitting, or I would have had to jump into another one like a squirrel. But people like me are nimble." Drawing his sword, he gave each one a few good blows to the chest, then went back to the horsemen and said, "The work is done. I finished off both of them, but it was hard. In their need they pulled up trees to defend themselves. But it didn't help them, not against someone like me who kills seven with one blow."

"Are you not wounded?" asked the horsemen.

"Everything is all right," answered the tailor. "They did not so much as bend one of my hairs."

Not wanting to believe him, the horesemen rode into the woods. There they found the giants swimming in their own blood, and all around lay the uprooted trees. The little tailor asked the king for the promised reward, but the latter regretted the promise, and once again he began to think of a way to get the hero off his neck.

"Before you receive my daughter and half the kingdom," he said, "you must fulfill another heroic deed. In the woods there is a unicorn that is causing much damage. First you must capture it.

"I am even less afraid of a unicorn than I was of two giants. Seven with one blow, that is my thing." Taking a rope and an ax, he went into the woods. Once again he told those who went with him to wait behind.

He did not have to look very long. The unicorn soon appeared, leaping toward the tailor as if it wanted to spear him at once.

"Gently, gently," said the tailor. "Not so fast." He stopped, waited until the animal was very near, then jumped agilely behind a tree. The unicorn ran with all its might into the tree, sticking its horn so tightly into the trunk that it did not have enough strength to pull it out again, and thus it was captured.

"Now I have the little bird," said the tailor, coming out from behind the tree. First he tied the rope around the unicorn's neck, then he cut the horn out of the tree with the ax. When everything was ready, he led the animal away and brought it to the king.

The king still did not want to give him the promised reward and presented a third requirement. Before the wedding, the tailor was to capture a wild boar that was causing great damage in the woods. Huntsmen were to assist him.

"Gladly," said the tailor. "That is child's play." He did not take the huntsmen into woods with him, and they were glad about that, for they had encountered the wild boar before and had no desire to do so again.

When the boar saw the tailor he ran toward him with foaming mouth and grinding teeth, wanting to throw him to the ground. But the nimble hero ran into a nearby chapel, then with one leap jumped back out through a window. The boar ran in after him, but the tailor ran around outside and slammed the door. Thus the furious animal was captured, for it was too heavy and clumsy to jump out the window. The little tailor called to the huntsmen. They had to see the captured boar with their own eyes.

The hero reported to the king, who now—whether he wanted to or not—had to keep his promise and give him his daughter and half the kingdom. If he had known that it was not a war hero, but rather a little tailor standing before him, it would have been even more painful for him. The wedding was thus held with great ceremony but little joy, and a king was made from a tailor. Some time later the young queen heard in the night how her husband said in a dream, "Boy, make the jacket for me,

and patch the trousers, or I will hit you across your ears with a yardstick."

Thus she determined where the young lord had come from. The next morning she brought her complaint to her father, asking him to help her get rid of the man, who was nothing more than a tailor.

The king comforted her, saying, "Tonight leave your bedroom door unlocked. My servants will stand outside, and after he falls asleep they will go inside, bind him, and carry him to a ship that will take him far away from here." The wife was satisfied with this. However, the king's squire, who had a liking for the young lord, heard everything and revealed the whole plot to him.

"I'll put a stop to that," said the little tailor. That evening he went to bed with his wife at the usual time. When she thought he was asleep she got up, opened the door, and then went back to bed. The little tailor, who was only pretending to be asleep, began crying out with a clear voice, "Boy, make the jacket for me, and patch the trousers, or I will hit you across your ears with a yardstick! I have struck down seven with one blow, killed two giants, led away a unicorn, and captured a wild boar, and I am supposed to be afraid of those who are standing just outside the bedroom!"

When those standing outside heard the tailor say this, they were so overcome with fear that they ran away, as though the wild horde was behind them. None of them dared to approach him ever again. Thus the little tailor was a king, and he remained a king as long as he lived.

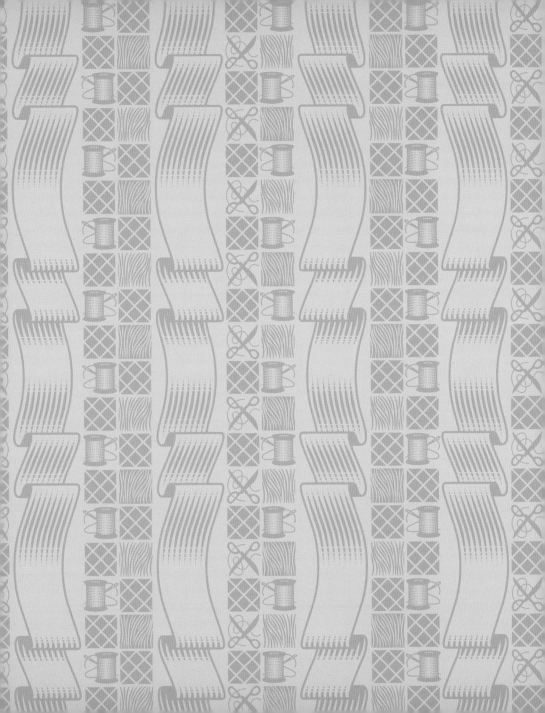

THE
OLD
WOMAN
IN THE
FOREST

 poor servant-girl was once travelling with the family with which she was in service, through a great forest, and when they were in the midst of it, robbers came out of the thicket, and murdered all they found. All perished together except the girl, who had jumped out of the carriage in a fright, and hidden herself behind a tree.

When the robbers had gone away with their booty, she came out and beheld the great disaster. Then she began to weep bitterly, and said, "What can a poor girl like me do now? I do not know how to get out of the forest, no human being lives in it, so I must certainly starve." She walked about and looked for a road, but could find none. When it was evening she seated herself under a tree, gave herself into God's keeping, and resolved to sit waiting there and not go away, let what might happen.

When, however, she had sat there for a while, a white dove came flying to her with a little golden key in its mouth. It put the little key in her hand, and said, "Dost thou see that great tree, therein is a little lock, it opens with the tiny key, and there thou wilt find food enough, and suffer no more hunger." Then she went to the tree and opened it, and found milk in a little dish, and white bread to break into it, so that she could eat her fill.

When she was satisfied, she said, "It is now the time when the hens at home go to roost, I am so tired I could go to bed too." Then the dove flew to her again, and brought another golden key in its bill, and said, "Open that tree there, and thou willt find a bed." So she opened it, and found a beautiful white bed, and she prayed God to protect her during the night, and lay down and slept.

In the morning the dove came for the third time, and again brought a little key, and said, "Open that tree there, and thou wilt find clothes." And when she opened it, she found garments beset with gold and with jewels, more splendid than those of any king's daughter. So she lived there for some time, and the dove came every day and provided her with all she needed, and it was a quiet good life.

Once, however, the dove came and said, "Wilt thou do something for my sake?"

"With all my heart," said the girl.

Then said the little dove, "I will guide thee to a small house; enter it, and inside it, an old woman will be sitting by the fire and will say, 'Good-day.' But on thy life give her no answer, let her do what she will, but pass by her on the right side; further on, there is a door, which open, and thou wilt enter into a room where a quantity of rings of all kinds are lying, amongst which are some magnificent ones with shining stones; leave them, however, where they are, and seek out a plain one, which must likewise be amongst them, and bring it here to me as quickly as thou canst."

The girl went to the little house, and came to the door. There sat an old woman who stared when she saw her, and said, "Good-day my child." The girl gave her no answer, and opened the door.

"Whither away," cried the old woman, and seized her by the gown, and wanted to hold her fast, saying, "That is my house; no one can go in there if I choose not to allow it."

But the girl was silent, got away from her, and went straight into the room. Now there lay on the table an enormous quantity of rings, which gleamed and glittered before her eyes. She turned them over and looked for the plain one, but could not find it. While she was seeking, she saw the old woman and how she was stealing away, and wanting to get off with a

bird-cage which she had in her hand. So she went after her and took the cage out of her hand, and when she raised it up and looked into it, a bird was inside which had the plain ring in its bill. Then she took the ring, and ran quite joyously home with it, and thought the little white dove would come and get the ring, but it did not.

Then she leant against a tree and determined to wait for the dove, and, as she thus stood, it seemed just as if the tree was soft and pliant, and was letting its branches down. And suddenly the branches twined around her, and were two arms, and when she looked round, the tree was a handsome man, who embraced and kissed her heartily, and said, "Thou hast delivered me from the power of the old woman, who is a wicked witch. She had changed me into a tree, and every day for two hours I was a white dove, and so long as she possessed the ring I could not regain my human form."

Then his servants and his horses, who had likewise been changed into trees, were freed from the enchantment also, and stood beside him. And he led them forth to his kingdom, for he was a King's son, and they married, and lived happily.

LITTLE SNOW WHITE

Once upon a time in midwinter, when the snowflakes were falling like feathers from heaven, a queen sat sewing at her window, which had a frame of black ebony wood. As she sewed she looked up at the snow and pricked her finger with her needle. Three drops of blood fell into the snow. The red on the white looked so beautiful that she thought to herself, "If only I had a child as white as snow, as red as blood, and as black as the wood in this frame."

Soon afterward she had a little daughter who was as white as snow, as red as blood, and as black as ebony wood, and therefore they called her Little Snow-White. And as soon as the child was born, the queen died.

A year later the king took himself another wife. She was a beautiful woman, but she was proud and arrogant, and she could not stand it if anyone might surpass her in beauty. She had a magic mirror. Every morning she stood before it, looked at herself, and said:

Mirror, mirror, on the wall,
Who in this land is fairest of all?

To this the mirror answered: You, my queen, are fairest of all.

Then she was satisfied, for she knew that the mirror spoke the truth.

Snow-White grew up and became ever more beautiful. When she was seven years old she was as beautiful as the light of day, even more beautiful than the queen herself.

One day when the queen asked her mirror:

Mirror, mirror, on the wall,
Who in this land is fairest of all?

It answered:

You, my queen, are fair; it is true.
But Snow-White is a thousand times
fairer than you.

The queen took fright and turned yellow and green with envy. From that hour on whenever she looked at Snow-White her heart turned over inside her body, so great was her hatred for the girl. The envy and pride grew ever greater, like a weed in her heart, until she had no peace day and night.

Then she summoned a huntsman and said to him, "Take Snow-White out into the woods. I never want to see her again. Kill her, and as proof that she is dead bring her lungs and her liver back to me."

The huntsman obeyed and took Snow-White into the woods. He took out his hunting knife and was about to stab it into her innocent heart when she began to cry, saying, "Oh, dear huntsman, let me live. I will run into the wild woods and never come back."

Because she was so beautiful the huntsman took pity on her, and he said, "Run away, you poor child."

He thought, "The wild animals will soon devour you anyway," but still it was as if a stone had fallen from his heart, for he would not have to kill her.

Just then a young boar came running by. He killed it, cut out its lungs and liver, and took them back to the queen as proof of Snow-White's death. The cook had to boil them

with salt, and the wicked woman ate them, supposing that she had eaten Snow-White's lungs and liver.

The poor child was now all alone in the great forest, and she was so afraid that she just looked at all the leaves on the trees and did not know what to do. Then she began to run. She ran over sharp stones and through thorns, and wild animals jumped at her, but they did her no harm. She ran as far as her feet could carry her, and just as evening was about to fall she saw a little house and went inside in order to rest.

Inside the house everything was small, but so neat and clean that no one could say otherwise. There was a little table with a white tablecloth and seven little plates, and each plate had a spoon, and there were seven knives and forks and seven mugs as well. Against the wall there were seven little beds, all standing in a row and covered with snow-white sheets.

Because she was so hungry and thirsty Snow-White ate a few vegetables and a little bread from each little plate, and from each mug she drank a drop of wine. Afterward, because she was so tired, she lay down on a bed, but none of them felt right—one was too long, the other too short—until finally the seventh one was just right. She remained lying in it, entrusted herself to God, and fell asleep.

After dark the masters of the house returned home. They were the seven dwarfs who picked and dug for ore in the mountains. They lit their seven candles, and as soon as it was light in their house they saw that someone had been there, for not everything was in the same order as they had left it.

The first one said, "Who has been sitting in my chair?"

The second one, "Who has been eating from my plate?"

The third one, "Who has been eating my bread?"

The fourth one, "Who has been eating my vegetables?"

The fifth one, "Who has been sticking with my fork?"

The sixth one, "Who has been cutting with my knife?"

The seventh one, "Who has been drinking from my mug?"

Then the first one saw a that there was a little imprint in his bed, and said, "Who stepped on my bed?"

The others came running up and shouted, "Someone has been lying in mine as well."

But the seventh one, looking at his bed, found Snow-White lying there asleep. The seven dwarfs all came running up, and they cried out with amazement. They fetched their seven candles and shone the light on Snow-White. "Oh good heaven! Oh good heaven!" they cried. "This child is so beautiful!"

They were so happy, that they did not wake her up, but let her continue to sleep there in the bed. The seventh

dwarf had to sleep with his companions, one hour with each one, and then the night was done.

The next morning Snow-White woke up, and when she saw the seven dwarfs she was frightened. But they were friendly and asked, "What is your name?"

"My name is Snow-White," she answered.

"How did you find your way to our house?" the dwarfs asked further. Then she told them that her step-mother had tried to kill her, that the huntsman had spared her life, and that she had run the entire day, finally coming to their house.

The dwarfs said, "If you will keep house for us, and cook, make beds, wash, sew, and knit, and keep everything clean and orderly, then you can stay with us, and you shall have everything that you want."

"Yes," said Snow-White, "with all my heart."

So she kept house for them. Every morning they went into the mountains looking for ore and gold, and in the evening when they came back home their meal had to be ready. During the day the girl was alone.

The good dwarfs warned her, saying, "Be careful about your stepmother. She will soon know that you are here. Do not let anyone in."

Now the queen, believing that she had eaten Snow-White's lungs and liver, could only think that she was again the first and the most beautiful woman of all. She stepped before her mirror and said:

Mirror, mirror, on the wall,
Who in this land is fairest of all?

It answered:

You, my queen, are fair; it is true.
But Snow-White, beyond the mountains
With the seven dwarfs,
Is still a thousand times fairer than you:

This startled the queen, for she knew that the mirror did not lie, and she realized that the huntsman had deceived her, and that Snow-White was still alive. Then she thought, and thought again, how she could kill Snow-White, for as long as she was not the most beautiful woman in the entire land her envy would give her no rest.

At last she thought of something. Coloring her face, she disguised herself as an old peddler woman, so that no one would recognize her. In this disguise she went to the house of the seven dwarfs. Knocking on the door she called out, "Beautiful wares for sale, for sale!"

Snow-White peered out the window and said, "Good day, dear woman, what do you have for sale?"

"Good wares, beautiful wares," she answered. "Bodice laces in all colors." And she took out one that was braided from colorful silk. "Would you like this one?"

"I can let that honest woman in," thought Snow-White, then unbolted the door and bought the pretty bodice lace.

"Child," said the old woman, "how you look! Come, let me lace you up properly."

The unsuspecting Snow-White stood before her and let her do up the new lace, but the old woman pulled so quickly and so hard that Snow-White could not breathe. "You used to be the most beautiful one," said the old woman, and hurried away.

Not long afterward, in the evening time, the seven dwarfs came home. How terrified they were when they saw their dear Snow-White lying on the ground, not moving at all, as though she were dead. They lifted her up, and, seeing that she was too tightly laced, they cut the lace in two. Then she began to breathe a little, and little by little she came back to life.

When the dwarfs heard what had happened they said, "The old peddler woman was no one else but the godless queen. Take care and let no one in when we are not with you."

When the wicked woman returned home she went to her mirror and asked:

Mirror, mirror, on the wall,
Who in this land is fairest of all?

The mirror answered once again:

You, my queen, are fair; it is true.
But Snow-White, beyond the mountains
With the seven dwarfs,
Is still a thousand times fairer
than you.

When she heard that, all her blood ran to her heart because she knew that Snow-White had come back to life.

"This time," she said, "I shall think of something that will destroy you."

Then with the art of witchcraft, which she understood, she made a poisoned comb. Then she disguised herself, taking the form of a different old woman. Thus she went across the seven mountains to the seven dwarfs, knocked on the door, and called out, "Good wares for sale, for sale!"

Snow-White looked out and said, "Go on your way. I am not allowed to let anyone in."

"You surely may take a look," said the old woman, pulling out the poisoned comb and holding it up. The child liked it so much that she let herself be deceived, and she opened the door.

After they had agreed on the purchase, the old woman said, "Now let me comb your hair properly."

She had barely stuck the comb into Snow-White's hair when the poison took effect, and the girl fell down unconscious.

"You specimen of beauty," said the wicked woman, "now you are finished." And she walked away.

Fortunately it was almost evening, and the seven dwarfs came home. When they saw Snow-White lying on the ground as if she were dead, they immediately suspected her stepmother. They examined her and found the poisoned comb.

They had scarcely pulled it out when Snow-White came to herself again and told them what had happened. Once again they warned her to be on guard and not to open the door for anyone.

Back at home the queen stepped before her mirror and said:

Mirror, mirror, on the wall,
Who in this land is fairest of all?

The mirror answered:

You, my queen, are fair; it is true.
But Snow-White, beyond the mountains
With the seven dwarfs,
Is still a thousand times fairer than you.

When the queen heard the mirror saying this, she shook and trembled with anger, "Snow-White shall die," she shouted, "if it costs me my life!"

Then she went into her most secret room—no one else was allowed inside—and she made a poisoned, poisoned apple. From the outside it was beautiful, white with red cheeks, and anyone who saw it would want it. But anyone who might eat a little piece of it would die. Then, coloring her face, she disguised herself as a peasant woman, and thus went across the seven mountains to the seven dwarfs. She knocked on the door.

Snow-White stuck her head out the window and said, "I am not allowed to let anyone in. The dwarfs have forbidden me to do so."

"That is all right with me," answered the peasant woman. "I'll easily get rid of my apples. Here, I'll give you one of them."

"No," said Snow-White, "I cannot accept anything."

"Are you afraid of poison?" asked the old woman. "Look, I'll cut the apple in two. You eat the red half, and I shall eat the white half."

Now the apple had been so artfully made that only the red half was poisoned. Snow-White longed for the

beautiful apple, and when she saw that the peasant woman was eating part of it she could no longer resist, and she stuck her hand out and took the poisoned half. She barely had a bite in her mouth when she fell to the ground dead.

The queen looked at her with a gruesome stare, laughed loudly, and said, "White as snow, red as blood, black as ebony wood! This time the dwarfs cannot awaken you."

Back at home she asked her mirror:

Mirror, mirror, on the wall,
Who in this land is fairest of all?

It finally answered:

You, my queen, are fairest of all.

Then her envious heart was at rest, as well as an envious heart can be at rest.

When the dwarfs came home that evening they found Snow-White lying on the ground. She was not breathing at all. She was dead. They lifted her up and looked for something

poisonous. They undid her laces. They combed her hair. They washed her with water and wine. But nothing helped. The dear child was dead, and she remained dead. They laid her on a bier, and all seven sat next to her and mourned for her and cried for three days. They were going to bury her, but she still looked as fresh as a living person, and still had her beautiful red cheeks.

They said, "We cannot bury her in the black earth," and they had a transparent glass coffin made, so she could be seen from all sides. They laid her inside, and with golden letters wrote on it her name, and that she was a princess. Then they put the coffin outside on a mountain, and one of them always stayed with it and watched over her. The animals too came and mourned for Snow-white, first an owl, then a raven, and finally a dove.

Snow-White lay there in the coffin a long, long time, and she did not decay, but looked like she was asleep, for she was still as white as snow and

as red as blood, and as black-haired as ebony wood.

Now it came to pass that a prince entered these woods and happened onto the dwarfs' house, where he sought shelter for the night. He saw the coffin on the mountain with beautiful Snow-White in it, and he read what was written on it with golden letters.

Then he said to the dwarfs, "Let me have the coffin. I will give you anything you want for it."

But the dwarfs answered, "We will not sell it for all the gold in the world."

Then he said, "Then give it to me, for I cannot live without being able to see Snow-White. I will honor her and respect her as my most cherished one."

As he thus spoke, the good dwarfs felt pity for him and gave him the coffin. The prince had his servants carry it away on their shoulders. But then it happened that one of them stumbled on some brush, and this dislodged from Snow-White's throat the piece of poisoned apple that she had bitten off. Not long afterward she opened her eyes, lifted the lid from her coffin, sat up, and was alive again.

"Good heavens, where am I?" she cried out.

The prince said joyfully, "You are with me." He told her what had happened, and then said, "I love you more than anything else in the world. Come with me to my father's castle. You shall become my wife." Snow-White loved him, and she went with him. Their wedding was planned with great splendor and majesty.

Snow-White's godless stepmother was also invited to the feast. After putting on her beautiful clothes she stepped before her mirror and said:

Mirror, mirror, on the wall,
Who in this land is fairest of all?

The mirror answered:

You, my queen, are fair; it is true.
But the young queen is a thousand times fairer than you.

The wicked woman uttered a curse, and she became so frightened, that she did not know what to do. At first she did not want to go to the wedding, but she found no peace. She had to go and see the young queen. When she arrived she recognized Snow-White, and terrorized, she could only stand there without moving.

Then they put a pair of iron shoes into burning coals. They were brought forth with tongs and placed before her. She was forced to step into the red-hot shoes and dance until she fell down dead.

THE
STRANGE
MUSICIAN

Once upon a time there was a strange musician who was walking through the woods all by himself, thinking about this and that. When there was nothing left for him to think about, he said to himself, "It is boring here in the woods. I am going to get myself a good companion." Then he took his fiddle from his back, and played a tune that sounded through the trees.

Before long a wolf came trotting through the thicket toward him. "Ah, a wolf is coming. I have no desire for him," said the musician, but the wolf came nearer and said to him, "Ah, dear musician, you play very well. I too would like to learn to play."

"You can learn quickly," answered the musician. "You will only have to do what I tell you."

"Oh, musician," said the wolf, "I will obey you like a pupil obeys his teacher." The musician told him to come along with him, and when they had walked some distance together, they came to an old oak tree. It was hollow inside and split up the middle.

"Look," said the musician, "if you want learn to play the fiddle, put your forepaws into this crack." The wolf obeyed, and the musician quickly picked up a stone, and with one blow wedged his two paws so firmly that he had to stay lying there like a prisoner. "Wait here until I return," said the musician, and went on his way.

After a while he again said to himself, "It is boring here in the woods. I will get myself another companion." He took his fiddle and again played into the woods. Before long a fox came creeping through the trees toward him. "Ah, a fox is coming," said the musician. "I have no desire for him."

The fox came up to him and said,

"Oh, dear musician, you play very well. I too would like to learn to play."

"You can learn quickly," said the musician. "You will only have to do what I tell you."

"Oh, musician," answered the fox, "I will obey you like a pupil obeys his teacher."

"Follow me," said the musician, and when they had gone some distance together, they came to a footpath with tall saplings on both sides. There the musician stood still, and from one side he bent a young hazelnut tree down to the ground and put his foot on the end of it. Then he bent down another young tree from the other side, and said, "Now little fox, if you want to learn something, give me your left front paw." The fox obeyed, and the musician tied his paw to the left stem. "Little fox," he said, "now give me your right paw." He tied this one to the right stem. After making sure that the knots in the cord were tight enough, he let go. The trees sprang upright and jerked the little fox upward, leaving him hanging there struggling in the air.

"Wait here until I return," said the musician, and went on his way.

Once again he said to himself, "It is boring here in the woods. I will get myself another companion. So he took his fiddle, and music sounded through the woods. Then a little hare came jumping toward him. "Ah, a hare is coming," said the musician. "I do not want him."

"Oh, dear musician," said the hare, "You play very well. I too would like to learn to play."

"You can learn quickly," said the musician. "You will only have to do what I tell you."

"Oh, musician," replied the little hare, "I will obey you like a pupil obeys his teacher." When they had gone some distance together, they came to an aspen tree in a clearing in the woods. The musician tied a long string around the little hare's neck, then tied the other end of the string to the tree.

"Now quickly, little hare, run twenty times around the tree," shouted the musician, and the little hare obeyed. When he had run around twenty times, he had wound the string twenty times around the trunk of the tree, and the little hare was caught. The more the hare tugged and pulled, the more the string cut into his tender neck. "Wait here until I return," said the musician, and went on his way.

The wolf, in the meantime, had pushed and pulled and bitten at the stone, and had worked so long that he freed his feet from the crack. Full of anger and rage he rushed after the musician, wanting to tear him to pieces. When the fox saw him running by, he began to wail, crying out with all his might, "Brother wolf, come help me. The musician has tricked me." The wolf pulled down the trees, bit the cord in two, and freed the fox, who went with him to take revenge on the musician. They found the tied-up hare, whom they rescued as well, then all together they set forth to find their enemy.

The musician had played his fiddle once again as he went on his way, and this time he had been more fortunate. The sound reached the ears of a poor woodcutter, who instantly, whether he wanted to or not, stopped working and, with his ax under his arm, came toward the musician to listen to the music.

"At last the right companion is coming," said the musician, "for I was seeking a human being, not wild animals." And he began to play so beautifully and delightfully that the poor man stood there enraptured, his heart filled with pleasure.

While he was thus standing there, the wolf, the fox, and the hare approached. He saw well that they had evil intentions, so he raised his shining axe and placed himself before the musician, as if to say, "Anyone who wants to harm him beware, for he will have to deal with me." Then the beasts took fright and ran back into the woods. The musician, however, played one more tune for the man to thank him, and then went on his way.

THE SPIRIT IN THE GLASS BOTTLE

Once upon a time there was a poor woodcutter who worked from morning until late at night. When he had finally saved up some money he said to his boy, "You are my only child. I want to spend the money that I have earned by the sweat of my brow on your education. Learn an honest trade so you can support me in my old age when my limbs have grown stiff and I have to sit at home."

Then the boy went to a university and studied diligently. His teachers praised him, and he remained there for some time. After he had worked through a few classes, but was still not perfect in everything, the little pittance that the father had saved was all spent, and the boy had to return home to him.

"Oh," said the father sadly, "I cannot give you anything more, and in these hard times I cannot earn a heller more than what we need for our daily bread."

"Father, dear," answered the son, "don't worry about it. If it is God's will everything will turn out well for me. I will do all right."

When the father said he was going into the woods and earn some money by cutting cordwood, the son said, "I will go with you and help you."

"No, my son," said the father, "you will find it too difficult. You are not used to hard work, and will not be able to do it. Furthermore, I have only one ax and no money left to buy another one with."

"Just go to the neighbor," answered the son. "He will lend you his ax until I have earned enough to buy one for myself."

So the father borrowed an ax from the neighbor, and the next morning at daybreak they went out into the woods together. The son helped his father and was quite cheerful and full of energy. When the sun was directly above them, the father said, "Let us rest now and eat our noon meal. Then all will go twice as well."

The son picked up his bread and said, "Just you rest, father. I am not tired. I will walk about a little in the woods and look for birds' nests."

"Oh, you fool," said the father, "why do you want to run about? Afterwards you will be tired and no longer able to lift an arm. Stay here, and sit down beside me."

But the son went into the woods, ate his bread, was very cheerful, and looked into the green branches to see if he could find a bird's nest. He walked to and fro until at last he came to an enormous oak that was certainly many hundred years old, and that five men would not have been able to span. He stood there looking at it, and thought, "Many a bird must have built its nest in that tree."

Then suddenly he thought that he heard a voice. Listening, he became aware of someone calling out with a muffled voice, "Let me out. Let me out."

He looked around but could not see anything. Then he thought that the voice was coming out of the ground, so he shouted, "Where are you?"

The voice answered, "I am stuck down here among the oak roots. Let me out. Let me out."

The student began to scrape about beneath the tree, searching among the roots, until at last he found a glass bottle in a little opening. Lifting it up, he held it against the light, and then saw something shaped like a frog jumping up and down inside.

"Let me out. Let me out," it cried again, and the student, thinking no evil, pulled the cork from the bottle. Immediately a spirit ascended from it and began to grow. It grew so fast that within a few moments a horrible fellow, half as big as the tree, was standing there before the student.

"Do you know," he cried in an terrifying voice, "what your reward is for having let me out?"

"No," replied the student fearlessly. "How should I know that?"

"Then I will tell you," shouted the spirit. "I must break your neck for it."

"You should have said so sooner," answered the student, "for then I would have left you shut up inside. However, my head is going to stay where it is until more people have been consulted."

"More people here, more people there," shouted the spirit. "You shall have the reward you have earned. Do you think that I was shut up there for such a long time as a favor? No, it was a punishment. I am the mighty Mercurius. I must break the neck of whomsoever releases me."

"Calm down," answered the student. "Not so fast. First I must know that you really were shut up in that little bottle, and that you are the right spirit. If you can indeed get inside again, then I will believe it, and you may do with me whatsoever you want."

The spirit said arrogantly, "that is an easy trick," pulling himself in and making himself as thin and short as he had been before. He then crept back into the opening and through the neck of the bottle. He was scarcely inside when the student pushed the cork back into the bottle, and threw it back where it had been among the oak roots. And thus the spirit was deceived.

The student was about to return to his father, but the spirit cried out pitifully, "Oh, do let me out. Oh, do let me out."

"No," answered the student, "not a second time. I will not release a person who once tried to kill me, now that I have captured him again."

"If you will set me free," cried the spirit, "I will give you so much that you will have enough for all the days of your life."

"No," answered the student, "you would cheat me like you tried to the first time."

"You are giving away your own good fortune," said the spirit. "I will not harm you, but instead will reward you richly."

The student thought, "I will venture it. Perhaps he will keep his word, and in any event he will not get the better of me." So he pulled out the cork, and the spirit rose up from the bottle as before, and extended himself, becoming as large as a giant.

"Now you shall have your reward," he said, handing the student a little rag that looked just like a small bandage. He said, "If you rub a wound with the one end, it will heal, and if you rub steel or iron with the other end, it will turn into silver."

"I have to try that," said the student. He went to a tree, scratched the bark with his ax, then rubbed it with the one end of the bandage. It immediately closed together and was healed.

"Now it is all right," he said to the spirit, "and we can part."

The spirit thanked him for having freed him, and the student thanked the spirit for the present, and returned to his father.

"Where have you been running about?" said the father. "Why have you forgotten your work? I said that you wouldn't get anything done."

"Don't be concerned, father. I will make it up."

"Make it up indeed," said the father angrily. "Don't bother."

"Just watch, father. I will soon cut down that tree there and make it crash."

Then he took his bandage, rubbed the ax with it, and struck a mighty blow, but because the iron had turned into silver, the cutting edge bent back on itself. "Hey, father, just look what a bad ax you've given me. It is all bent out of shape."

The father was shocked and said, "Oh, what have you done! Now I'll have to pay for the ax, and I don't know what with. That is all the good I have from your work."

"Don't get angry," said the son, "I will pay for the ax."

"Oh, you blockhead," cried the father, "How will you pay for it? You have nothing but what I give you. You have students' tricks stuck in your head, but you don't know anything about chopping wood."

After a little while the student said, "Father, I can't work any longer after all. Let's quit for the day."

"Now then," he answered, "do you think I can stand around with my hands in my pockets like you? I have to go on working, but you may head for home."

"Father, I am here in these woods for the first time. I don't know my way alone. Please go with me." His anger had now subsided, so the father at last let himself be talked into going home with him.

There he said to the son, "Go and sell the damaged ax and see what you can get for it. I will have to earn the difference, in order to pay the neighbor."

The son picked up the ax and took it into town to a goldsmith, who tested it, weighed it, and then said, "It is worth four hundred talers. I do not have that much cash with me."

The student said, "Give me what you have. I will lend you the rest."

The goldsmith gave him three hundred talers and owed him one hundred.

Then the student went home and said, "Father, I have some money. Go and ask the neighbor what he wants for the ax."

"I already know," answered the old man. "One taler, six groschens."

"Then give him two talers, twelve groschens. That is double its worth and is plenty. See, I have more than enough money." Then he gave the father a hundred talers, saying, "You shall never need anything. Live just like you want to."

"My goodness," said the old man. "Where did you get all that money?"

Then the son told him everything that had happened, and how by trusting in his luck he had made such a catch. With the money that was left he went back to the university and continued his studies, and because he could heal all wounds with his bandage he became the most famous doctor in the whole world.

THE
TURNIP

There were once two brothers who both served as soldiers; one of them was rich, and the other poor. Then the poor one, to escape from his poverty, put off his soldier's coat, and turned farmer. He dug and hoed his bit of land, and sowed it with turnip-seed. The seed came up, and one turnip grew there which became large and vigorous, and visibly grew bigger and bigger, and seemed as if it would never stop growing, so that it might have been called the princess of turnips, for never was such an one seen before, and never will such an one be seen again.

At length it was so enormous that by itself it filled a whole cart, and two oxen were required to draw it, and the farmer had not the least idea what he was to do with the turnip, or whether it would be a fortune to him or a misfortune. At last he thought, "If thou sellest it, what wilt thou get for it

that is of any importance, and if thou eatest it thyself, why, the small turnips would do thee just as much good; it would be better to take it to the King, and make him a present of it."

So he placed it on a cart, harnessed two oxen, took it to the palace, and presented it to the King. "What strange thing is this?" said the King. "Many wonderful things have come before my eyes, but never such a monster as this! From what seed can this have sprung, or are you a luck-child and have met with it by chance?" — "Ah, no!" said the farmer, "no luck-child am I. I am a poor soldier, who because he could no longer support himself hung his soldier's coat on a nail and took to farming land. I have a brother who is rich and well known to you, Lord King, but I, because I have nothing, am forgotten by every one."

Then the King felt compassion for him, and said, "Thou shalt be raised from thy poverty, and shalt have such gifts from me that thou shalt be equal to thy rich brother." Then he bestowed on him much gold, and lands, and meadows, and herds, and made him immensely rich, so that the wealth of the other brother could not be compared with his. When the rich brother heard what the poor one had gained for himself with one single turnip, he envied him, and thought in every way how he also could get hold of a similar piece of luck. He would, however, set about it in a much wiser way, and took gold and horses and carried them to the King, and made certain the King would give him a much larger present in return. If his brother had got so much for one turnip, what would he not carry away with him in return for such beautiful things as these?

The King accepted his present, and said he had nothing to give him in return that was more rare and excellent than the great turnip. So the rich man was obliged to put his brother's turnip in a cart and have it taken to his home. When there he did not know on whom to vent his rage and anger, until bad thoughts came to him, and he resolved to kill his brother. He hired murderers, who were to lie in ambush, and then he went to his brother and said, "Dear brother, I know of a hidden treasure, we will dig it up together, and divide it between us." The other agreed to this, and accompanied him without suspicion.

While they were on their way, however, the murderers fell on him, bound him, and would have hanged him to a tree. But just as they were doing this, loud singing and the sound of a horse's feet were heard in the distance. On this their hearts were filled with terror, and they pushed their prisoner head first into the sack, hung it on a branch, and took to flight. He, however, worked up there until he had made a hole in the sack through which he could put his head. The man who was coming by was no other than a travelling student, a young fellow who rode on his way through the wood joyously singing his song. When he who was aloft saw that someone was passing below him, he cried, "Good day! You have come at a lucky time." The student looked round on every side, but did not know whence the voice came. At last he said, "Who calls me?" Then an answer came from the top of the tree, "Raise your eyes; here I sit aloft in the Sack of Wisdom. In a short time have I learnt great things; compared with this all schools are a jest; in a very short time I shall have learnt everything, and shall descend wiser than all other men. I understand the stars, and the signs of the Zodiac, and the tracks of the winds, the sand of the sea, the healing of illness, and the virtues of all herbs, birds, and stones. If you were once within it you would feel what noble things issue forth from the Sack of Knowledge."

The student, when he heard all this, was astonished, and said, "Blessed be the hour in which I have found thee! May not I also enter the sack for a while?" He who was above replied as if unwillingly, "For a short time I will let you get into it, if you reward me and give me good words; but you must wait an hour longer, for one thing remains which I must learn before I do it." When the student had waited a while he became impatient, and begged to be allowed to get in at once, his thirst for knowledge was so very great. So he who was above pretended at last to yield, and said, "In order that I may come forth from the house of knowledge you must let it down by the rope, and then you shall enter it." So the student let the sack down, untied it, and set him free, and then cried, "Now draw me up at once," and was about to get into the sack. "Halt!" said the other, "that won't do," and took him by the head and put him upside down into the sack, fastened it, and drew the disciple of wisdom up the tree by the rope. Then he swung him in the air and said, "How goes it with thee, my dear fellow? Behold, already thou feelest wisdom coming, and art gaining valuable experience. Keep perfectly quiet until thou becomest wiser." Thereupon he mounted the student's horse and rode away, but in an hour's time sent some one to let the student out again.

THE KING OF THE GOLDEN MOUNTAIN

REX AUERI MONTIS

There was once a merchant who had only one child, a son, that was very young, and barely able to run alone. He had two richly laden ships then making a voyage upon the seas, in which he had embarked all his wealth, in the hope of making great gains, when the news came that both were lost. Thus from being a rich man he became all at once so very poor that nothing was left to him but one small plot of land; and there he often went in an evening to take his walk, and ease his mind of a little of his trouble.

One day, as he was roaming along in a brown study, thinking with no great comfort on what he had been and what he now was, and was like to be, all on a sudden there stood before him a little, rough-looking, black dwarf. 'Prithee, friend, why so sorrowful?' said he to the merchant; 'what is it you take so deeply to heart?'

'If you would do me any good I would willingly tell you,' said the merchant.

'Who knows but I may?' said the little man: 'tell me what ails you, and perhaps you will find I may be of some use.' Then the merchant told him how all his wealth was gone to the bottom of the sea, and how he had nothing left but that little plot of land. 'Oh, trouble not yourself about that,' said the dwarf; 'only undertake to bring me here, twelve years hence, whatever meets you first on your going home, and I will give you as much as you please.'

The merchant thought this was no great thing to ask; that it would most likely be his dog or his cat, or something of that sort, but forgot his little boy Heinel; so he agreed to the bargain, and signed and sealed the bond to do what was asked of him.

But as he drew near home, his little boy was so glad to see him that he crept behind him, and laid fast hold of his legs, and looked up in his face and laughed. Then the father started trembling with fear and horror, and saw what it was that he had bound himself to do; but as no gold was come, he made himself easy by thinking that it was only a joke that the dwarf was playing him, and that, at any rate, when the money came, he should see the bearer, and would not take it in.

About a month afterwards he went upstairs into a lumber-room to look for some old iron, that he might sell it and raise a little money; and there, instead of his iron, he saw a large pile of gold lying on the floor. At the sight of this he was overjoyed, and forgetting all about his son, went into trade again, and became a richer merchant than before.

Meantime little Heinel grew up, and as the end of the twelve years drew near the merchant began to call to mind his bond, and became very

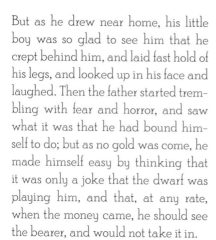

sad and thoughtful; so that care and sorrow were written upon his face. The boy one day asked what was the matter, but his father would not tell for some time; at last, however, he said that he had, without knowing it, sold him for gold to a little, ugly-looking, black dwarf, and that the twelve years were coming round when he must keep his word. Then Heinel said, 'Father, give yourself very little trouble about that; I shall be too much for the little man.'

When the time came, the father and son went out together to the place agreed upon: and the son drew a circle on the ground, and set himself and his father in the middle of it. The little black dwarf soon came, and walked round and round about the circle, but could not find any way to get into it, and he either could not, or dared not, jump over it. At last the boy said to him, 'Have you anything to say to us, my friend, or what do you want?'

Now Heinel had found a friend in a good fairy, that was fond of him, and had told him what to do; for this fairy knew what good luck was in store for him. 'Have you brought me what you said you would?' said the dwarf to the merchant.

The old man held his tongue, but Heinel said again, 'What do you want here?'

The dwarf said, 'I come to talk with your father, not with you.'

'You have cheated and taken in my father,' said the son; 'pray give him up his bond at once.'

'Fair and softly,' said the little old man; 'right is right; I have paid my money, and your father has had it, and spent it; so be so good as to let me have what I paid it for.'

'You must have my consent to that first,' said Heinel, 'so please to step in here, and let us talk it over.' The old man grinned, and showed his teeth, as if he should have been very glad to get into the circle if he could.

Then at last, after a long talk, they came to terms. Heinel agreed that his father must give him up, and that so far the dwarf should have his way: but, on the other hand, the fairy had told Heinel what fortune was in store for him, if he followed his own course; and he did not choose to be given up to his hump-backed friend, who seemed so anxious for his company.

So, to make a sort of drawn battle of the matter, it was settled that Heinel should be put into an open boat that lay on the sea-shore hard by; that the father should push him off with his own hand, and that he should thus be set adrift, and left to the bad or good luck of wind and weather.

Then he took leave of his father, and set himself in the boat, but before it got far off a wave struck it, and it fell with one side low in the water, so the merchant thought that poor Heinel was lost, and went home very sorrowful, while the dwarf went his way, thinking that at any rate he had had his revenge.

The boat, however, did not sink, for the good fairy took care of her friend, and soon raised the boat up again, and it went safely on. The young man sat safe within, till at length it ran ashore upon an unknown land. As he jumped upon the shore he saw before him a beautiful castle but empty and dreary within, for it was enchanted. 'Here,' said he to himself, 'must I find the prize the good fairy told me of.' So he once more searched the whole palace through, till at last he found a white snake, lying coiled up on a cushion in one of the chambers.

Now the white snake was an enchanted princess; and she was very glad to see him, and said, 'Are you at last come to set me free? Twelve long years have I waited here for the fairy to bring you hither as she promised, for you alone can save me. This night twelve men will come: their faces will be black, and they will be dressed in chain armour. They will ask what you do here, but give no answer; and let them do what they will—beat, whip, pinch, prick, or torment you—bear all;

only speak not a word, and at twelve o'clock they must go away. The second night twelve others will come: and the third night twenty-four, who will even cut off your head; but at the twelfth hour of that night their power is gone, and I shall be free, and will come and bring you the Water of Life, and will wash you with it, and bring you back to life and health.'

And all came to pass as she had said; Heinel bore all, and spoke not a word; and the third night the princess came, and fell on his neck and kissed him. Joy and gladness burst forth throughout the castle, the wedding was celebrated, and he was crowned king of the Golden Mountain.

They lived together very happily, and the queen had a son. And thus eight years had passed over their heads, when the king thought of his father; and he began to long to see him once again. But the queen was against his going, and said, 'I know well that misfortunes will come upon us if you go.'

However, he gave her no rest till she agreed. At his going away she gave him a wishing-ring, and said, 'Take this ring, and put it on your finger; whatever you wish it will bring you; only promise never to make use of it to bring me hence to your father's house.' Then he said he would do what she asked, and put the ring on his finger, and wished himself near the town where his father lived.

Heinel found himself at the gates in a moment; but the guards would not let him go in, because he was so strangely clad. So he went up to a neighbouring hill, where a shepherd dwelt, and borrowed his old frock, and thus passed unknown into the town. When he came to his father's house, he said he was his son; but the merchant would not believe him, and said he had had but one son, his poor Heinel, who he knew was long since dead: and as he was only dressed like a poor shepherd, he would not even give him anything to eat. The king, however, still vowed that he was his son, and said, 'Is there no mark by which you would know me if I am really your son?'

'Yes,' said his mother, 'our Heinel had a mark like a raspberry on his right arm.' Then he showed them the mark, and they knew that what he had said was true.

He next told them how he was king of the Golden Mountain, and was married to a princess, and had a son seven years old. But the merchant said, 'that can never be true; he must be a fine king truly who travels about in a shepherd's frock!'

At this the son was vexed; and forgetting his word, turned his ring, and wished for his queen and son. In an instant they stood before him; but the queen wept, and said he had broken his word, and bad luck would follow. He did all he could to soothe her, and she at last seemed to be appeased; but she was not so in truth, and was only thinking how she should punish him.

One day he took her to walk with him out of the town, and showed her the spot where the boat was set adrift upon the wide waters. Then he sat himself down, and said, 'I am very much tired; sit by me, I will rest my head in your lap, and sleep a while.'

As soon as he had fallen asleep, however, she drew the ring from his finger, and crept softly away, and wished herself and her son at home in their kingdom. And when he awoke he found himself alone, and saw that the ring was gone from his finger. 'I can never go back to my father's house,' said he; 'they would say I am a sorcerer: I will journey forth into the world, till I come again to my kingdom.'

So saying he set out and travelled till he came to a hill, where three giants were sharing their father's goods; and as they saw him pass they cried out and said, 'Little men have sharp wits; he shall part the goods between us.'

Now there was a sword that cut off an enemy's head whenever the wearer gave the words, 'Heads off!'; a cloak that made the owner invisible, or gave him any form he pleased; and a pair of boots that carried the wearer wherever he wished.

Heinel said they must first let him try these wonderful things, then he might know how to set a value upon them. Then they gave him the cloak, and he wished himself a fly, and in a moment he was a fly. 'The cloak is very well,' said he: 'now give me the sword.'

'No,' said they; 'not unless you undertake not to say, "Heads off!" for if you do we are all dead men.' So they gave it him, charging him to try it on a tree. He next asked for the boots also; and the moment he had all three in his power, he wished himself at the Golden Mountain; and there he was at once. So the giants were left behind with no goods to share or quarrel about.

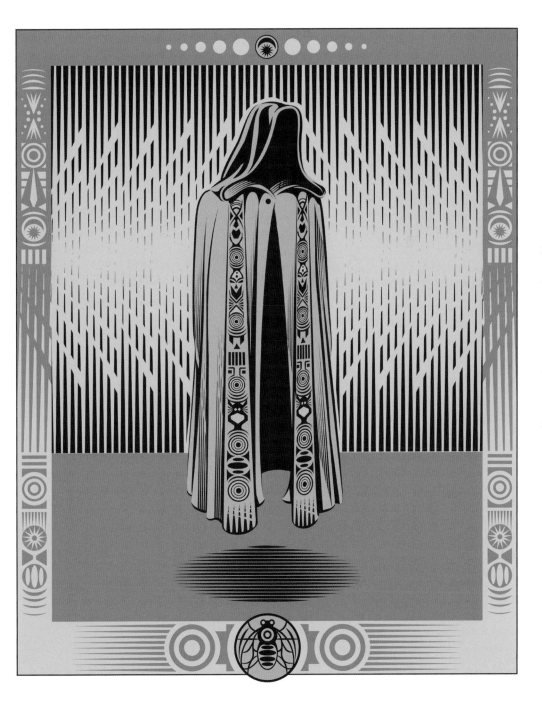

As Heinel came near his castle he heard the sound of merry music; and the people around told him that his queen was about to marry another husband. Then he threw his cloak around him, and passed through the castle hall, and placed himself by the side of the queen, where no one saw him. But when anything to eat was put upon her plate, he took it away and ate it himself; and when a glass of wine was handed to her, he took it and drank it; and thus, though they kept on giving her meat and drink, her plate and cup were always empty.

Upon this, fear and remorse came over her, and she went into her chamber alone, and sat there weeping; and he followed her there. 'Alas!' said she to herself, 'was I not once set free? Why then does this enchantment still seem to bind me?'

'False and fickle one!' said he. 'One indeed came who set thee free, and he is now near thee again; but how have you used him? Ought he to have had such treatment from thee?'

Then he went out and sent away the company, and said the wedding was at an end, for that he was come back to the kingdom. But the princes, peers, and great men mocked at him. However, he would enter into no parley with them, but only asked them if they would go in peace or not.

Then they turned upon him and tried to seize him; but he drew his sword. 'Heads Off!' cried he; and with the word the traitors' heads fell before him, and Heinel was once more king of the Golden Mountain.

THE FROG KING

OR

IRON HEINRICH

In olden times, when wishing still did some good, there lived a king whose daughters were all beautiful, but the youngest was so beautiful that the sun itself, who, indeed, has seen so much, marveled every time it shone upon her face. In the vicinity of the king's castle there was a large, dark forest, and in this forest, beneath an old linden tree, there was a well. In the heat of the day the princess would go out into the forest and sit on the edge of the cool well. To pass the time she would take a golden ball, throw it into the air, and then catch it. It was her favorite plaything.

Now one day it happened that the princess's golden ball did not fall into her hands, that she held up high, but instead it fell to the ground and rolled right into the water. The princess followed it with her eyes, but the ball disappeared, and the well was so deep that she could not see its bottom.

Then she began to cry. She cried louder and louder, and she could not console herself.

As she was thus lamenting, someone called out to her, "What is the matter with you, princess? Your crying would turn a stone to pity."

She looked around to see where the voice was coming from and saw a frog, who had stuck his thick, ugly head out of the water. "Oh, it's you, old water-splasher," she said. "I am crying because my golden ball has fallen into the well."

"Be still and stop crying," answered the frog. I can help you, but what will you give me if I bring back your plaything?"

"Whatever you want, dear frog," she said, "my clothes, my pearls and precious stones, and even the golden crown that I am wearing."

The frog answered, "I do not want your clothes, your pearls and precious stones, nor your golden crown, but if you will love me and accept me as a companion and playmate, and let me sit next to you at your table and eat from your golden plate and drink from your cup and sleep in your bed, if you will promise this to me, then I'll dive down and bring your golden ball back to you."

"Oh, yes," she said, "I promise all of that to you if you will just bring the ball back to me." But she thought, "What is this stupid frog trying to say? He just sits here in the water with his own kind and croaks. He cannot be a companion to a human."

As soon as the frog heard her say "yes" he stuck his head under and dove to the bottom. He paddled back up a short time later with the golden ball in his mouth and threw it onto the grass.

The princess was filled with joy when she saw her beautiful plaything once again, picked it up, and ran off.

"Wait, wait," called the frog, "take me along. I cannot run as fast as you." But what did it help him, that he croaked out after her as loudly as he could? She paid no attention to him, but instead hurried home and soon forgot the poor frog, who had to return again to his well.

The next day the princess was sitting at the table with the king and all the people of the court, and was eating from her golden plate when something came creeping up the marble steps: plip, plop, plip, plop. As soon as it reached the top, there came a knock at the door, and a voice called out, "Princess, youngest, open the door for me!"

She ran to see who was outside. She opened the door, and the frog was sitting there. Frightened, she slammed the door shut and returned to the table. The king saw that her heart was pounding and asked, "My child, why are you afraid? Is there a giant outside the door who wants to get you?"

"Oh, no," she answered. "it is a disgusting frog."

"What does the frog want from you?"

"Oh, father dear, yesterday when I was sitting near the well in the forest and playing, my golden ball fell into the water. And because I was crying so much, the frog brought it back, and because he insisted, I promised him that he could be my companion, but I didn't think that he could leave his water. But now he is just outside the door and wants to come in."

Just then there came a second knock at the door, and a voice called out:

Youngest daughter of the king,
Open up the door for me,
Don't you know what yesterday,
You said to me down by the well?
Youngest daughter of the king,
Open up the door for me.

The king said, "What you have promised, you must keep. Go and let the frog in."

She went and opened the door, and the frog hopped in, then followed her up to her chair. He sat there and called out, "Lift me up next to you."

She hesitated, until finally the king commanded her to do it.

When the frog was seated next to her he said, "Now push your golden plate closer, so we can eat together."

She did it, but one could see that she did not want to. The frog enjoyed his meal, but for her every bite stuck in her throat.

Finally he said, "I have eaten all I want and am tired. Now carry me to your room and make your bed so that we can go to sleep."

The princess began to cry and was afraid of the cold frog and did not dare to even touch him, and yet he was supposed to sleep in her beautiful, clean bed.

The king became angry and said, "You should not despise someone who has helped you in time of need."

She picked him up with two fingers, carried him upstairs, and set him in a corner. As she was lying in bed, he came creeping up to her and said, "I am tired, and I want to sleep as well as you do. Pick me up or I'll tell your father."

With that she became bitterly angry and threw him against the wall with all her might. "Now you will have your peace, you disgusting frog!"

But when he fell down, he was not a frog, but a prince with beautiful friendly eyes. And he was now, according to her father's will, her dear companion and husband. He told her how he had been enchanted by a wicked witch, and that she alone could have rescued him from the well, and that tomorrow they would go together to his kingdom. Then they fell asleep. The next morning, just as the sun was waking them, a carriage pulled up, drawn by eight horses. They had white ostrich feathers on their heads and were outfitted with chains of gold. At the rear stood the young king's servant, faithful Heinrich. Faithful Heinrich had been so saddened by his master's transformation into a frog that he had had to place three iron bands around his heart to keep it from bursting in grief and sorrow.

The carriage was to take the king back to his kingdom. Faithful Heinrich lifted them both inside and took his place at the rear. He was filled with joy over the redemption. After they had gone a short distance, the prince heard a crack from behind, as though something had broken. He turned around and said, "Heinrich, the carriage is breaking apart."

No, my lord, the carriage it's not,
But one of the bands surrounding my heart,
That suffered such great pain,
When you were sitting in the well,
When you were a frog.

Once again, and then once again the prince heard a cracking sound and thought that the carriage was breaking apart, but it was the bands springing from faithful Heinrich's heart because his master was now redeemed and happy.

THE MAGIC TABLE

THE GOLDEN DONKEY

AND THE CUDGEL IN THE SACK

There was once upon a time a tailor who had three sons, and only one goat. But as the goat supported all of them with her milk, she was obliged to have good food, and to be taken every day to pasture. The sons did this, in turn.

Once the eldest took her to the churchyard, where the finest herbs were to be found, and let her eat and run about there. At night when it was time to go home he asked, "Goat, have you had enough?"

The goat answered,
I have eaten so much,
Not a leaf more I'll touch;
Meh, meh!

"Come home, then," said the youth, and took hold of the cord around her neck, led her into the stable, and tied her up securely.

"Well," said the old tailor, "has the goat had as much food as she ought?"

"Oh," answered the son, "she has eaten so much, not a leaf more she'll touch."

But the father wished to satisfy himself, and went down to the stable, stroked the dear animal, and asked, "Goat, are you satisfied?"

The goat answered,
How should I be satisfied?
Among the ditches I leapt about,
Found no leaf, so went without;
Meh, meh!

"What do I hear?" cried the tailor, and ran upstairs and said to the youth, "Hey, you liar, you said the goat had had enough, and have let her hunger." And in his anger he took the yardstick from the wall, and drove him out with blows.

Next day it was the turn of the second son, who sought a place next to the garden hedge where nothing but good herbs grew, and the goat gobbled them all up. At night when he wanted to go home, he asked, "Goat, are you satisfied?"

I have eaten so much,
Not a leaf more I'll touch;
Meh, meh!

"Come home then," said the youth, and led her home, and tied her up in the stable.

"Well," said the old tailor, "has the goat had as much food as she ought?"

"Oh," answered the son, "she has eaten so much, not a leaf more she'll touch."

The tailor would not rely on this, but went down to the stable and said, "Goat, have you had enough?"

The goat answered,
How should I be satisfied?

Meh! Meh!

Among the ditches I leapt about,
Found no leaf, so went without;
Meh, meh!

"The godless wretch!" cried the tailor, to let such a good animal hunger, and he ran up and drove the youth out of doors with the yardstick.

Now came the turn of the third son, who wanted to do his duty well, and sought out some bushes with the finest leaves, and let the goat devour them. In the evening when he wanted to go home, he asked, "Goat, have you had enough?"

The goat answered,
I have eaten so much,
Not a leaf more I'll touch;
Meh, meh!

"Come home then," said the youth, and led her into the stable, and tied her up.

"Well," said the old tailor, "has the goat had her full share of food?"

"She has eaten so much, not a leaf more she'll touch."

The tailor was distrustful, went down, and asked, "Goat, have you had enough?"

The wicked beast answered,
How should I be satisfied?
Among the ditches I leapt about, Found no leaf, so went without; Meh, meh!

"Oh, the brood of liars!" cried the tailor, "Each as wicked and forgetful of his duty as the other. You shall no longer make a fool of me!" And quite beside himself with anger, he ran upstairs and tanned the poor young fellow's back so vigorously with the yardstick that he leaped out of the house.

The old tailor was now alone with his goat. Next morning he went down into the stable, stroked the goat and said, "Come, my dear little animal, I myself will take you to feed." He took her by the rope and led her to green hedges, and amongst yarrow and whatever else goats like to eat. "Here you may for once eat to your heart's content," he said to her, and let her browse till evening. Then he asked, "Goat, are you satisfied?"

She answered,
I have eaten so much,
Not a leaf more I'll touch;
Meh, meh!

"Come home then," said the tailor, and led her into the stable, and tied her fast. When he was going away, he turned around again and said, "Well, are you satisfied for once?"

But the goat behaved no better for him, and cried,
How should I be satisfied?
Among the ditches I leapt about, Found no leaf, so went without; Meh, meh!

When the tailor heard that, he was shocked, and saw clearly that he had driven away his three sons without

cause. "Wait, you ungrateful creature," he cried, "it is not enough to drive you away, I will brand you so that you will no more dare to show yourself amongst honest tailors."

He quickly ran upstairs, fetched his razor, lathered the goat's head, and shaved her as clean as the palm of his hand. And as the yardstick would have been too honorable for her, he grabbed a whip, and gave her such blows with it that she bounded away with tremendous leaps.

When the tailor was thus left quite alone in his house he fell into great grief, and would gladly have had his sons back again, but no one knew where they were gone.

The eldest had apprenticed himself to a joiner, and learned industriously and tirelessly, and when the time came for him to be on his way, his master presented him with a little table which was not particularly beautiful, and was made of common wood, but which had one good property. If anyone set it out, and said,

"table be set," the good little table was at once covered with a clean little cloth, and a plate was there, and a knife and fork beside it, and dishes with boiled meats and roasted meats, as many as there was room for, and a great glass of red wine shone, so that it made the heart glad.

The young journeyman thought, "With this you have enough for your whole life," and went joyously about the world and never troubled himself at all whether an inn was good or bad, or if anything was to be found in it or not. When it suited him, he did not enter an inn at all, but either on the plain, in a wood, a meadow, or wherever he fancied, he took his little table off his back, set it down before him, and said, "table be set," and then everything appeared that his heart desired.

At length he took it into his head to go back to his father, whose anger would now be appeased, and who would now willingly receive him with his magic table. It came to pass that on his way home, he came one

evening to an inn which was filled with guests. They bade him welcome, and invited him to sit and eat with them, for otherwise he would have difficulty in getting anything.

"No," answered the joiner, "I will not take the few morsels out of your mouths. Rather than that, you shall be my guests."

They laughed, and thought he was jesting with them. He but placed his wooden table in the middle of the room, and said, "Table be set." Instantly it was covered with food, so good that the host could never have procured it, and the smell of it ascended pleasantly to the nostrils of the guests.

"Fall to, dear friends," said the joiner, and the guests when they saw that he meant it, did not need to be asked twice, but drew near, pulled out their knives and attacked it valiantly. And what surprised them the most was that when a dish became empty, a full one instantly took its place of its own accord.

The innkeeper stood in one corner and watched the affair. He did not at all know what to say, but thought, "You could easily find a use for such a cook as that in your household."

The joiner and his comrades made merry until late into the night. At length they lay down to sleep, and the young journeyman also went to bed, and set his magic table against the wall. The host's thoughts, however, let him have no rest.

It occurred to him that there was a little old table in his backroom which looked just like the journeyman's and he brought it out, and carefully exchanged it for the wishing table. Next morning the joiner paid for his bed, took up his table, never thinking that he had got a false one, and went his way.

At midday he reached his father, who received him with great joy. "Well, my dear son, what have you learned?" he said to him.

"Father, I have become a joiner."

"A good trade," replied the old man. "But what have you brought back with you from your apprenticeship?"

"Father, the best thing which I have brought back with me is this little table."

The tailor inspected it on all sides and said, "You did not make a masterpiece when you made this. It is a bad old table."

"But it is a table-be-set," replied the son. "When I set it out, and tell it to set itself, the most beautiful dishes immediately appear on it, and wine also, which gladdens the heart. Just invite all our relatives and friends. They shall refresh and enjoy themselves for once, for the table will fill them all."

When the company was assembled, he put his table in the middle of the room and said, "Table be set," but the little table did not move, and remained just as bare as any other table which does not understand language. Then the poor journeyman became aware

that his table had been changed, and was ashamed at having to stand there like a liar. The relatives, however, mocked him, and were forced to go home without having eaten or drunk.

The father brought out his scraps again, and went on tailoring, but the son found work with a master joiner.

The second son had gone to a miller and had apprenticed himself to him. When his years were over, the master said, "As you have conducted yourself so well, I give you a donkey of a peculiar kind, which neither draws a cart nor carries a sack."

"What good is he then?" asked the young journeyman.

"He spews forth gold," answered the miller. "If you set him on a cloth and say 'Bricklebrit,' the good animal will spew forth gold pieces for you from back and front."

"That is a fine thing," said the journeyman, and thanked the master, and went out into the world. When he had need of gold, he had only to

say "Bricklebrit" to his donkey, and it rained gold pieces, and he had nothing to do but pick them off the ground. Wherever he went, the best of everything was good enough for him, and the more expensive the better, for he had always a full purse. When he had looked about the world for some time, he thought, "You must seek out your father. If you go to him with the gold-donkey he will forget his anger, and receive you well."

It came to pass that he came to the same inn in which his brother's table had been exchanged. He led his donkey by the bridle, and the host was about to take the animal from him and tie him up, but the young journeyman said, "Don't trouble yourself, I will take my nag into the stable, and tie him up myself too, for I must know where he is."

This struck the host as odd, and he thought that a man who was forced to look after his donkey himself, could not have much to spend. But when the stranger put his hand in his pocket and brought out two gold pieces, and said he was to provide something good for him, the host opened his eyes wide, and ran and sought out the best he could muster. After dinner the guest asked what he owed. The innkeeper did not see why he should not double the bill, and said the journeyman must give two more gold pieces. He felt in his pocket, but his gold was just at an end.

"Wait an instant, sir," said he, "I will go and fetch some money." But he took the tablecloth with him. The innkeeper could not imagine what this meant, and being curious, stole after him, and as the guest bolted the stable door, he peeped through a hole left by a knot in the wood.

The stranger spread out the cloth under the animal and cried, "Bricklebrit," and immediately the beast began to let gold pieces fall from back and front, so that it fairly rained down money onto the ground.

"Eh, my word," said the innkeeper. "Ducats are quickly coined there. A purse like that is not bad." The guest

paid his bill and went to bed, but in the night the innkeeper stole down into the stable, led away the master of the mint, and tied up another donkey in his place.

Early next morning the journeyman traveled away with his donkey, and thought that he had his gold-donkey. At midday he reached his father, who rejoiced to see him again, and gladly took him in.

"What have you made of yourself, my son?" asked the old man.

"A miller, dear father," he answered.

"What have you brought back with you from your travels."

"Nothing else but a donkey."

"There are donkeys enough here," said the father, "I would rather have had a good goat."

"Yes," replied the son, "but it is no common donkey, but a gold-donkey. When I say 'Bricklebrit' the good beast spews forth a whole sheetful of gold pieces. Just summon all our relatives here, and I will make them rich folks."

"That suits me well," said the tailor, "for then I shall have no need to torment myself any longer with the needle," and he himself ran out and called the relatives together. As soon as they were assembled, the miller bade them make way, spread out his cloth, and brought the donkey into the room.

"Now watch," said he, and cried, "Bricklebrit," but what fell were not gold pieces, and it was clear that the animal knew nothing of the art, for not every donkey attains such perfection. Then the poor miller made a long face, saw that he had been betrayed, and begged pardon of the relatives, who went home as poor as they came. There was no help for it, the old man had to take up his needle once more, and the youth hired himself to a miller.

The third brother had apprenticed himself to a turner, and as that is skilled labor, he was the longest in learning. His brothers, however, told him in a letter how badly things had gone with them, and how the innkeeper had cheated them of their beautiful wishing gifts on the last evening before they reached home. When the turner had served his time, and was about to set forth, as he had conducted himself so well, his master presented him with a sack saying, "There is a cudgel in it."

"I can take the sack with me," said he, "and it may serve me well, but why should the cudgel be in it. It only makes it heavy."

"I will tell you why," replied the master. "If anyone has done anything to injure you, do but say, 'Cudgel out of the sack,' and the cudgel will leap forth among the people, and play such a dance on their backs that they will not be able to stir or move for a week. And it will not quit until you say, 'Cudgel into the sack.'"

The journeyman thanked him, and put the sack on his back, and when anyone came too near him and wished to attack him, he said, "Cudgel out of the sack," and instantly the cudgel sprang out and beat the dust out of their coats and jackets, right on their backs, not waiting until they had taken them off, and it was done so quickly, that before anyone was aware, it was already his own turn.

In the evening the young turner reached the inn where his brothers had been cheated. He laid his sack on the table before him, and began to talk of all the wonderful things which he had seen in the world.

"Yes," said he, "table-be-sets, gold donkeys, and things of that kind—extremely good things which I by no means despise—but these are nothing in comparison with the treasure which I have obtained and am carrying about with me here in my sack."

The innkeeper pricked up his ears. "What in the world can that be?" he thought. "The sack must be filled with nothing but jewels. I ought to get them cheap too, for all good things come in threes."

When it was time for sleep, the guest stretched himself out on the bench, laying his sack beneath him for a pillow. When the innkeeper thought his guest was lying in a sound sleep, he went to him and pushed and pulled quite gently and carefully at the sack to see if he could possibly take it away and lay another in its place.

The turner, however, had been waiting for this for a long time, and now just as the innkeeper was about to give a hearty tug, he cried, "Cudgel out of the sack!"

Instantly the little cudgel came forth, and falling on the innkeeper gave him a sound thrashing. The innkeeper cried for mercy, but the louder he cried, the harder the cudgel beat the time on his back, until at length he fell to the ground exhausted.

Then the turner said, "If you do not give back the table-be-set and the gold-donkey, the dance shall start again from the beginning."

"Oh, no!" cried the innkeeper, quite humbly, "I will gladly give everything back, only make the accursed kobold creep back into the sack."

Then the journeyman said, "I will let mercy take the place of justice, but beware of getting into mischief again" Then he cried, "Cudgel into the sack," and let him rest.

Next morning the turner went home to his father with the table-be-set, and the gold-donkey. The tailor rejoiced when he saw him once more, and asked him likewise what he had learned in foreign parts. "Dear father," said he, "I have become a turner."

"A skilled trade," said the father. "What have you brought back with you from your travels?"

"A precious thing, dear father," replied the son, "a cudgel in the sack."

"What!" cried the father, "A cudgel! That's worth your trouble! From every tree you can cut yourself one."

"But not one like this, dear father. If I say, 'Cudgel out of the sack,' the cudgel springs out and leads any-one ill-disposed toward me a weary dance, and never stops until he lies on the ground and prays for fair weather. Look you, with this cudgel have I rescued the table-be-set and the gold-donkey which the thievish innkeeper took away from my broth-ers. Now let them both be sent for, and invite all our relatives. I will give them to eat and to drink, and will fill their pockets with gold as well."

The old tailor had not much confi-dence. Nevertheless he summoned the relatives together. Then the turner spread a cloth in the room and led in the gold-donkey, and said to his brother, "Now, dear brother, speak to him."

The miller said, "Bricklebrit," and instantly the gold pieces rained down on the cloth like a cloudburst, and the donkey did not stop until every one of them had so much that he could carry no more. (I can see by your face that you would have liked to be there as well.)

Then the turner brought out the little table and said, "Now, dear brother, speak to it." And scarcely had the joiner said, "Table be set," than it was spread and amply covered with the most exquisite dishes. Then such a meal took place as the good tailor had never yet known in his house, and the whole party of relatives stayed together until after nightfall, and were all merry and glad.

The tailor locked his needle and thread and yardstick and pressing iron into a chest, and lived with his three sons in joy and splendor.

What, however, happened to the goat who was to blame for the tailor driving out his three sons? That I will tell you.

She was ashamed that she had a bald head, and ran to a fox's hole and crept into it. When the fox came home, he was met by two great eyes shining out of the darkness, and was terrified and ran away. A bear met him, and as the fox looked quite disturbed, he said, "What is the matter with you, Brother Fox, why do you look like that?"

"Ah," answered Redskin, "a fierce beast is in my cave and stared at me with its fiery eyes."

"We will soon drive him out," said the bear, and went with him to the cave and looked in, but when he saw the fiery eyes, fear seized on him likewise. He would have nothing to do with the furious beast, and took to his heels.

The bee met him, and as she saw that he was ill at ease, she said, "Bear, you are really pulling a very pitiful face. What has become of all your cheerfulness?"

"It is all very well for you to talk," replied the bear. "A furious beast with staring eyes is in Redskin's house, and we can't drive him out."

The bee said, "Bear, I pity you. I am a poor weak creature whom you would not turn aside to look at, but still, I believe I can help you." She flew into the fox's cave, lit on the goat's smoothly shorn head, and stung her so violently, that she sprang up, crying "meh, meh," and ran forth into the world as if mad, and to this hour no one knows where she has gone.

THE
OWL

wo or three hundred years ago, when people were far from being so crafty and cunning as they are nowadays, an extraordinary event took place in a little town. By some mischance one of the great owls, called horned owls, had come from the neighboring woods into the barn of one of the townsfolk in the night-time, and when day broke did not dare to venture forth again from her retreat, for fear of the other birds, which raised a terrible outcry whenever she appeared.

In the morning when the man-servant went into the barn to fetch some straw, he was so mightily alarmed at the sight of the owl sitting there in a corner, that he ran away and announced to his master that a monster, the like of which he had never set eyes on in his life, and which could devour a man without the slightest difficulty, was sitting in the barn, rolling its eyes about in its head.

"I know your kind," said the master, "you have courage enough to chase a blackbird about the fields, but when you see a hen lying dead, you have to get a stick before you go near it. I must go and see for myself what kind of a monster it is," added the master, and went quite boldly into the granary and looked round him. When, however, he saw with his own eyes the strange grim creature, he was no less terrified than the servant had been.

With two bounds he sprang out, ran to his neighbours, and begged them imploringly to lend him assistance against an unknown and dangerous beast, or else the whole town might be in danger if it were to break loose out of the barn, where it was shut up. A great noise and clamor arose in all the streets, the townsmen came armed with spears, hay-forks, scythes, and axes, as if they were going out against an enemy.

Finally, the senators appeared with the burgomaster at their head. When they had drawn up in the market-place, they marched to the barn, and surrounded it on all sides. Thereupon one of the most courageous of them stepped forth and entered with his spear lowered, but came running out immediately afterwards with a shriek and as pale as death, and could not utter a single word. Yet two others ventured in, but they fared no better.

At last one stepped forth, a great strong man who was famous for his warlike deeds, and said, "you will not drive away the monster by merely looking at him, we must be in earnest here, but I see that you have all tuned into women, and not one of you dares to encounter the animal." He ordered them to give him some armor, had a sword and spear brought, and armed himself. All praised his courage, though many feared for his life. The two barn-doors were opened, and they saw the owl, which in the meantime had perched herself on the middle of a great cross-beam. He had a ladder brought, and when he raised it, and made ready to climb up, they all cried out to him that he was to bear himself bravely, and commended him to St. George, who slew the dragon.

When he had just got to the top, and the owl perceived that he had designs on her, and was also bewildered by the crowd and the shouting, and knew not how to escape, she rolled her eyes, ruffled her feathers, flapped her wings, snapped her beak, and cried, tuwhit, tuwhoo, in a harsh voice. "Strike home. Strike home." Screamed the crowd outside to the valiant hero.

"Any one who was standing where I am standing," answered he, "would not cry, strike home." He certainly did plant his foot one rung higher on the ladder, but then he began to tremble, and half-fainting, went back again.

And now there was no one left who dared to place himself in such danger. The monster, said they, has poisoned and mortally wounded the very strongest man among us, by snapping at him and just breathing on him. Are we, too, to risk our lives. They took counsel as to what they ought to do to prevent the whole town from being destroyed. For a long time everything seemed to be of no use, but at length the burgomaster found an expedient.

"My opinion," said he, "is that we ought, out of the common purse, to pay for this barn, and whatsoever corn, straw, or hay it contains, and thus indemnify the owner, and then burn down the whole building and the terrible beast with it. Thus no one will have to endanger his life. This is no time for thinking of expense, and stinginess would be ill applied." All agreed with him. So they set fire to the barn at all four corners, and with it the owl was miserably burnt. Let any one who will not believe it, go thither and inquire for himself.

THE NIXIE IN THE POND

Once upon a time there was a miller. He lived contentedly with his wife. They had money and land, and their prosperity increased from year to year. But misfortune comes overnight. Just as their wealth had increased, so did it decrease from year to year, until finally the miller scarcely owned even the mill where he lived. He was in great distress, and when he lay down after a day's work, he found no rest, but tossed and turned in his bed, filled with worries.

One morning he got up before daybreak and went outside, thinking that the fresh air would lighten his heart. As he was walking across the mill dam, the first sunbeam was just appearing, and he heard something rippling in the pond. Turning around, he saw a beautiful woman rising slowly out of the water. Her long hair, which she was holding above her shoulders with her soft hands, flowed down on both sides, and covered her white body. He saw very well that she was the nixie of the pond, and he was so frightened that he did not know whether to run away or stay where he was. But the nixie, speaking with a soft voice, called him by name and asked him why he was so sad.

At first the miller was speechless, but when he heard her speak so kindly, he took heart and told her how he had lived with good fortune and wealth, but that now he was so poor that he did not know what to do.

"Be at ease," answered the nixie. "I will make you richer and happier than you have ever been before. You must only promise to give me that which has just been born in your house."

"What else can that be," thought the miller, "but a young dog or a young cat," and he promised her what she demanded. The nixie descended into the water again, and consoled and

in good spirits he hurried back to his mill. He had not yet arrived there when the maid came out of the front door and called out to him that he should rejoice, for his wife had given birth to a little boy.

The miller stood there as though he had been struck by lightning. He saw very well that the cunning nixie had known this and had cheated him. With his head lowered he went to his wife's bed. When she said, "Why are you not happy with the beautiful boy?" he told her what had happened to him, and what kind of a promise he had given to the nixie.

"What good to me are good fortune and prosperity," he added, "if I am to lose my child? But what can I do?" Even the relatives who had come to congratulate them did not have any advice for him.

In the meantime, good fortune returned to the miller's house. He succeeded in everything that he undertook. It was as though the trunks and strongboxes filled themselves of their own accord, and as though money in a chest multiplied overnight. Before long his wealth was greater than it had ever been before. However, it did not bring him happiness without concern, for his agreement with the nixie tormented his heart. Whenever he passed the pond he feared she might appear and demand payment of his debt.

He never allowed the boy himself to go near the water. "Beware!" he said to him. "If you touch the water a hand will appear, take hold of you, and pull you under."

However, year after year passed, and the nixie made no further appearance, so the miller began to feel at ease. The boy grew up to be a young man and was apprenticed to a huntsman. When he had learned this trade and had become a skilled huntsman, the lord of the village took him into his service.

In the village there lived a beautiful and faithful maiden whom the huntsman liked, and when his master noticed this, he gave him a little house. The two were married, lived

peacefully and happily, and loved each other sincerely.

One day the huntsman was pursuing a deer. When the animal ran out of the woods and into an open field he followed it and finally brought it down with a single shot. He did not notice that he was in the vicinity of the dangerous millpond, and after he had dressed out the deer, he went to the water in order to wash his bloodstained hands. However, he had scarcely dipped them into the water when the nixie emerged. Laughing, she wrapped her wet arms around him, then pulled him under so quickly that waves splashed over him.

When it was evening and the huntsman did not return home, his wife became frightened. She went out to look for him. He had often told her that he had to be on his guard against the nixie's snares, and that he did not dare to go near the millpond, so she already suspected what had happened. She hurried to the water, and when she found his hunting bag lying on the bank, she could no longer

have any doubt of the misfortune. Crying and wringing her hands, she called her beloved by name, but to no avail. She hurried across to the other side of the millpond, and called him anew. She cursed the nixie with harsh words, but no answer followed. The surface of the water remained calm; only the moon's half face stared steadily back up at her.

The poor woman did not leave the pond. With fast strides, never stopping to rest, she walked around it again and again, sometimes in silence, sometimes crying out loudly, sometimes sobbing softly. Finally her strength gave out, and she sank down to the ground, falling into a heavy sleep. She was soon immersed in a dream.

She was fearfully climbing upwards between large rocky cliffs. Thorns and briers were hacking at her feet. Rain was beating into her face. The wind was billowing her long hair about. When she reached the top a totally different sight presented itself to her. The sky was blue, a soft breeze was blowing, the ground sloped

gently downwards, and in a green meadow, dotted with colorful flowers, stood a neat cottage. She walked up to it and opened the door. There sat an old woman with white hair, who beckoned to her kindly.

At that moment, the poor woman awoke. It was already daylight, and she decided at once to follow her dream. With difficulty she climbed the mountain, and everything was just as she had seen it during the night. The old woman received her kindly, showing her a chair where she was to sit. "You must have met with misfortune," she said, "having sought out my lonely cottage."

The woman related with tears what had happened to her. "Be comforted," said the old woman. "I will help you. Here is a golden comb for you. Wait until the full moon has risen, then go to the millpond, sit down on the bank and comb your long black hair with this comb. When you are finished set it down on the bank, and you will see what will happen."

The woman returned home, but the time passed slowly for her until the full moon came. Finally the shining disk appeared in the heaven, and she went out to the millpond, sat down, and combed her long black hair with the golden comb. When she was finished she set it down at the water's edge. Before long there came a motion from beneath the water. A wave arose, rolled onto the bank, and carried the comb away with it. In not more time than it took for the comb to sink to the bottom, the surface of the water parted, and the huntsman's head emerged. He said nothing, only looking at his wife with sorrowful glances. That same instant a second wave rushed up and covered her husband's head. Then everything vanished. The millpond lay as peaceful as before, with only the face of the full moon shining on it.

Filled with sorrow, the woman returned, but she saw the old woman's cottage in a dream. The next morning she again set out and told her sorrows to the wise woman. The old woman

gave her a golden flute, and said, "Wait until the full moon comes again, then take this flute. Sit on the bank and play a beautiful tune on it. When you are finished set it in the sand. Then you will see what will happen."

The woman did what the old woman had told her to do. No sooner was the flute lying in the sand than there was a motion from beneath the water, and a wave rushed up and carried the flute away with it. Immediately afterwards the water parted, and not only her husband's head, but half of his body emerged as well. He stretched out his arms longingly towards her, but a second wave rushed up, covered him, and pulled him down again. "Oh, what does it help me," said the unhappy woman, "for me only to see my beloved and then to lose him again?"

Despair filled her heart anew, but a dream led her a third time to the old woman's house. She went there, and the wise woman gave her a golden spinning wheel, comforted her, and said, "Everything is not yet fulfilled.

Wait until the full moon comes, then take the spinning wheel, sit on the bank, and spin the spool full. When you have done this place the spinning wheel at the water's edge, and you will see what will happen."

The woman did everything exactly as she had been told. As soon as the full moon appeared she carried the golden spinning wheel to the bank, and span diligently until she was out of flax, and the spool was completely filled with thread. She had scarcely placed the wheel on the bank when there was a more violent motion than before from the water's depth. Then a powerful wave rushed up and carried the wheel away with it.

Immediately the head and the whole body of her husband emerged in a waterspout. He quickly jumped to the bank, caught his wife by the hand, and fled. They had gone only a little distance when the entire millpond arose with a terrible roar, then with terrible force streamed out across the countryside. The fugitives saw death before their eyes, when the wife in her

terror called out for the old woman to help them, and they were instantly transformed, she into a toad, he into a frog.

The flood which had overtaken them could not destroy them, but it separated them and carried them far away. When the water receded and they both reached dry land again, their human forms returned again, but neither knew where the other one was. They found themselves among strange people who did not know their native land. High mountains and deep valleys lay between them. In order to earn a living, they both had to herd sheep. For long years they drove their flocks through fields and woods, and were filled with sorrow and longing.

One day when spring had once again broken forth on the earth, they both went out with their flocks, and as chance would have it, they moved toward one another. He saw a herd on a distant mountainside and drove his sheep toward it. They met in a valley but did not recognize one another, but

they were happy that they were no longer so alone. From then on every day they drove their flocks next to each other. They did not speak much, but they did feel comforted.

One evening when the full moon was shining in the sky, and the sheep were already at rest, the shepherd took his flute out of his pocket and played on it a beautiful but sorrowful tune. When he had finished he saw that the shepherdess was crying bitterly. "Why are you crying? he asked.

"Oh," she answered, " the full moon was shining like this when I played that tune on the flute for the last time, and my beloved's head emerged out of the water."

He looked at her, and it was as though a veil fell from his eyes. He recognized his beloved wife, and when she looked at him, with the moon shining on his face, she recognized him as well. They embraced and kissed one another, and no one needs to ask if they were happy.

THE
MOUSE
THE
BIRD
AND THE
SAUSAGE

Once upon a time a mouse, a bird, and a sausage formed a partnership. They kept house together, and for a long time they lived in peace and prosperity, acquiring many possessions. The bird's task was to fly into the forest every day to fetch wood. The mouse carried water, made the fire, and set the table. The sausage did the cooking.

Whoever is too well off always wants to try something different! Thus one day the bird chanced to meet another bird, who boasted to him of his own situation. This bird criticized him for working so hard while the other two enjoyed themselves at home. For after the mouse had made the fire and carried the water, she could sit in the parlor and rest until it was time for her to set the table. The sausage had only to stay by the pot watching the food cook. When mealtime approached, she would slither through the porridge or the vegetables, and thus everything was greased and salted and ready to eat. The bird would bring his load of wood home. They would eat their meal, and then sleep soundly until the next morning. It was a great life.

The next day, because of his friend's advice, the bird refused to go to the forest, saying that he had been their servant long enough. He was no longer going to be a fool for them. Everyone should try a different task for a change. The mouse and the sausage argued against this, but the bird was the master, and he insisted that they give it a try. The sausage was to fetch wood, the mouse became the cook, and the bird was to carry water.

And what was the result? The sausage trudged off toward the forest; the bird made the fire; and the mouse put on the pot and waited for the sausage to return with wood for the next day. However, the sausage stayed out so long that the other two feared that something bad had happened. The bird flew off to see if he could find her. A short distance away he came upon a dog that had seized the sausage as free booty and was making off with her. The bird complained bitterly to the dog about this brazen abduction, but he claimed that he had discovered forged letters on the sausage, and that she would thus have to forfeit her life to him.

Filled with sorrow, the bird carried the wood home himself and told the mouse what he had seen and heard. They were very sad, but were determined to stay together and make the best of it. The bird set the table while the mouse prepared the food. She jumped into the pot, as the sausage had always done, in order to slither and weave in and about the vegetables and grease them, but before she reached the middle, her hair and skin were scalded off, and she perished.

When the bird wanted to eat, no cook was there. Beside himself, he threw the wood this way and that, called out, looked everywhere, but no cook was to be found. Because of his carelessness, the scattered wood caught fire, and the entire house was soon aflame. The bird rushed to fetch water, but the bucket fell into the well, carrying him with it, and he drowned.

LITTLE
RED
CAP

Once upon a time there was a sweet little girl. Everyone who saw her liked her, but most of all her grandmother, who did not know what to give the child next. Once she gave her a little cap made of red velvet. Because it suited her so well, and she wanted to wear it all the time, she came to be known as Little Red Cap.

One day her mother said to her, "Come Little Red Cap. Here is a piece of cake and a bottle of wine. Take them to your grandmother. She is sick and weak, and they will do her well. Mind your manners and give her my greetings. Behave yourself on the way, and do not leave the path, or you might fall down and break the glass, and then there will be nothing for your grandmother. And when you enter her parlor, don't forget to say 'Good morning,' and don't peer into all the corners first."

"I'll do everything just right," said Little Red Cap, shaking her mother's hand.

The grandmother lived out in the woods, a half hour from the village. When Little Red Cap entered the woods a wolf came up to her. She did not know what a wicked animal he was, and was not afraid of him.

"Good day to you, Little Red Cap."

"Thank you, wolf."

"Where are you going so early, Little Red Cap?"

"To grandmother's."

"And what are you carrying under your apron?"

"Grandmother is sick and weak, and I am taking her some cake and wine. We baked yesterday, and they should be good for her and give her strength."

"Little Red Cap, just where does your grandmother live?"

"Her house is good quarter hour from here in the woods, under the three large oak trees. There's a hedge of hazel bushes there. You must know the place," said Little Red Cap.

The wolf thought to himself, "Now that sweet young thing is a tasty bite for me. She will taste even better than the old woman. You must be sly, and you can catch them both."

He walked along a little while with Little Red Cap, then he said, "Little Red Cap, just look at the beautiful flowers that are all around us. Why don't you go and take a look? And I don't believe you can hear how beautifully the birds are singing. You are walking along as though you were on your way to school. It is very beautiful in the woods."

Little Red Cap opened her eyes and when she saw the sunbeams dancing to and fro through the trees and how the ground was covered with beautiful flowers, she thought, "If I take a fresh bouquet to grandmother, she will be very pleased. Anyway, it is still early, and I'll be home on time." And she ran off the path into the woods look-ing for flowers. Each time she picked one she thought that she could see an even more beautiful one a little way off, and she ran after it, going further and further into the woods. But the wolf ran straight to the grandmother's house and knocked on the door.

"Who's there?"

"Little Red Cap. I'm bringing you some cake and wine. Open the door."

"Just press the latch," called out the grandmother. "I'm too weak to get up."

The wolf pressed the latch, and the door opened. He stepped inside, went straight to the grandmother's bed, and ate her up. Then he put on her clothes, put her cap on his head, got into her bed, and pulled the curtains shut.

Little Red Cap had run after the flowers. After she had gathered so many that she could not carry any more, she remembered her grandmother, and then continued on her way to her house. She found, to her surprise, that the door was open. She walked into the parlor, and everything looked so strange that she thought, "Oh, my God, why am I so afraid? I usually like it at grandmother's."

She called out, "Good morning!" but received no answer.

Then she went to the bed and pulled back the curtains. Grandmother was lying there with her cap pulled down over her face and looking very strange.

"Oh, grandmother, what big ears you have!"

"All the better to hear you with."

"Oh, grandmother, what big eyes you have!"

"All the better to see you with."

"Oh, grandmother, what big hands you have!"

"All the better to grab you with!"

"Oh, grandmother, what a horribly big mouth you have!"

"All the better to eat you with!"

The wolf had scarcely finished speaking when he jumped from the bed with a single leap and ate up poor Little Red Cap. As soon as the wolf had satisfied his desires, he climbed back into bed, fell asleep, and began to snore very loudly.

A huntsman was just passing by. He thought, "The old woman is snoring so loudly. You had better see if something is wrong with her."

He stepped into the parlor, and when he approached the bed, he saw the wolf lying there. "So here I find you, you old sinner," he said. "I have been hunting for you a long time."

He was about to aim his rifle when it occurred to him that the wolf might have eaten the grandmother, and that she still might be rescued. So instead of shooting, he took a pair of scissors and began to cut open the wolf's belly. After a few cuts he saw the red cap shining through., and after a few more cuts the girl jumped out, crying, "Oh, I was so frightened! It was so dark inside the wolf's body!"

And then the grandmother came out as well, alive but hardly able to breathe. Then Little Red Cap fetched some large stones. She filled the wolf's body with them, and when he woke up and tried to run away, the stones were so heavy that he immediately fell down dead.

The three of them were happy. The huntsman skinned the wolf and went home with the pelt. The grandmother ate the cake and drank the wine that Little Red Cap had brought. And Little Red Cap thought, "As long as I live, I will never leave the path and run off into the woods by myself if mother tells me not to."

They also tell how Little Red Cap was taking some baked things to her grandmother another time, when another wolf spoke to her and wanted her to leave the path. But Little Red Cap took care and went straight to grandmother's. She told her that she had seen the wolf, and that he had wished her a good day, but had stared at her in a wicked manner. "If we hadn't been on a public road, he would have eaten me up," she said.

"Come," said the grandmother. "Let's lock the door, so he can't get in."

Soon afterward the wolf knocked on the door and called out, "Open up, grandmother. It's Little Red Cap, and I'm bringing you some baked things."

They remained silent, and did not open the door. Gray-Head crept around the house several times, and finally jumped onto the roof. He wanted to wait until Little Red Cap

went home that evening, then follow her and eat her up in the darkness. But the grandmother saw what he was up to. There was a large stone trough in front of the house.

"Fetch a bucket, Little Red Cap," she said to the child. "Yesterday I cooked some sausage. Carry the water that I boiled them with to the trough." Little Red Cap carried water until the large, large trough was clear full. The smell of sausage arose into the wolf's nose. He sniffed and looked down, stretching his neck so long that he could no longer hold himself, and he began to slide. He slid off the roof, fell into the trough, and drowned. And Little Red Cap returned home happily, and no one harmed her.

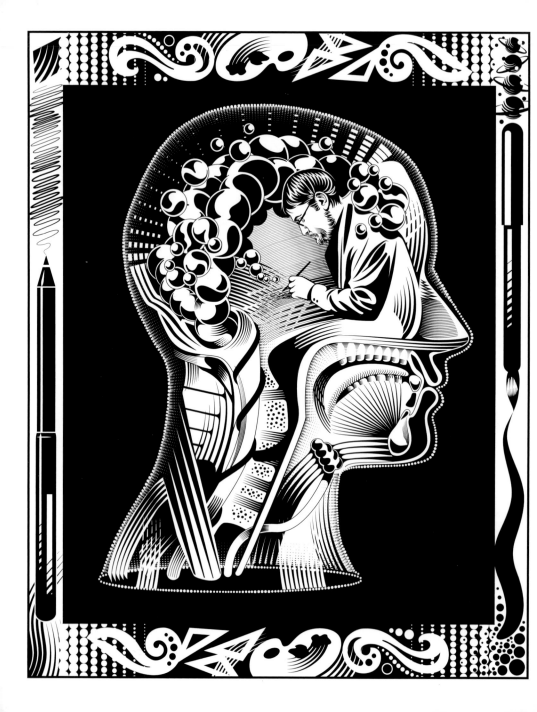

ABOUT YANN LEGENDRE

Yann Legendre is an internationally recognized illustrator, designer, and art director. His illustrations have appeared in the *Wall Street Journal*, *New York Times*, *GQ*, *Creative Review*, *Libération*, *The Guardian*, and numerous other publications He has worked regularly for Janus Films, Universal Music, The Criterion Collection, CB2, and many publishers to create illustrated film and theater posters, music CD collections, book covers, and collections of furniture. His work has been exhibited all across the world, including the United States, France, Japan, Finland, England, China, Bolivia, Mexico, Slovakia, Russia, Italy, Turkey, Bulgaria, and Poland.

In 2013, his illustrated book *Flesh Empire* received the Gold Medal at the 3x3 Professional Show, in New York, and his illustrated poster series for the Steppenwolf Theater, in Chicago, was awarded the Gold Pencil at the One Show. He is a member of the Society of Illustrators, in New York.

This reimagined edition of the classic favorite,
features 20 tales by the Brothers Grimm. Each
tale is accompanied by lush illustrations from
Yann Legendre. His surreal, sometimes haunting,
portrayals of the characters in Grimm's tales
are bold and utterly captivating, adding a new
depth to these classic characters.

This is just one in a new series of books from
Rockport Publishers. Classics Reimagined is a
library of stunning collector's editions of classic
novels illustrated by graphic artists and illustrators from around the world. Each artist offers
his or her own unique, visual interpretation of
the most well-loved, widely read, and avidly
collected literature from renowned authors.
From *The Wonderful Wizard of Oz* to *Sherlock
Holmes*, and from *Grimm's Fairy Tales* to
selected works from Edgar Allan Poe, art lovers
and book collectors alike will not be able to
resist owning the whole collection.

Also available
The Wonderful Wizard of Oz
978-1-59253-899-7

www.quartoknows.com